The Return
of
the Mahdi

A Novel

Sharon Alice Geyer

The Return of the Mahdi

Copyright © 2013 Sharon Alice Geyer

Scripture taken from the King James Version of the Bible

MEVASERET PRESS
ISBN-13: 978-0692240915
ISBN-10: 0692240918

Also by Sharon Alice Geyer

The Samson Option,
The Time of Jacob's Trouble

Non-fiction:
Daughter of Jerusalem,
An American Woman's
Journey of Faith

Dedicated to Jinous and Ainsley

You will arise and have mercy on Zion

For the time to favor her,

Yes, the set time, has come.

For your servants take pleasure

In her stones

And show favor to her dust.

Psalm 102:14-15

Prologue

The wind swept across the Sea of Galilee while the moon cast pale highlights on the choppy waves. Ari, in one end of the small fishing boat, faced his partner Shimon who sat opposite him. It was not Ari's nature to confide his inner thoughts to another person, not even to his beloved Lily. And yet, the atmosphere created by the semi-darkness, and the sound of the waves as they slapped against the wooden boat, lulled him into a sense of security. He instinctively felt Shimon, a gentle giant of a man, ten years older than himself, would not be put off by his confession.

Ari spoke in a stilted but modulated cadence about his abandonment at birth during the Six Day War, his upbringing by the kibbutz, the disastrous army service, and his eventual meeting with Lily. He then related how the Mahdi Brotherhood had kidnapped him and sequestered him in the *tekiyah* in Damascus. He spoke about an undercover mission to Tehran for the Mossad, even though he was sworn to secrecy on the subject.

"These Shi'ites believe I'm their Mahdi, the Muslim messiah. They believe I will restore the caliphate to them, and Jesus Christ will kneel to me. Crazy, huh?" Ari felt he had revealed too much, and held his breath as he waited for his partner's reaction.

After an awkward silence, Shimon lifted his head, pointed his bearded chin toward the sky and howled with laughter. He laughed so hard and long he soon put his hands to his ample belly to ease the ache.

"That's the strangest story. No kidding, an Israeli? The long awaited Mahdi?" Again, his body trembled with laughter.

Ari's facial muscles stiffened, as he made no attempt to hide his distress. "What's so hilarious?"

Shimon wiped the tears from his round cheeks with the back of his hand. "I know all about this so-called Holy One, the Twelfth Imam. I'm an Iraqi Jew by birth. Remember? We're familiar with Muslim theology. Our survival depended on us knowing our neighbors' mindset."

"Then tell me," Ari muttered, still not mollified. "What's so funny?"

"You!" Shimon made a half-hearted effort not to laugh again. Still smiling, he re-adjusted the nets in response to delicate changes in the water as schools of fish swarmed upward from the bottom of the lake.

Ari sniffed as though indifferent. "What do you know that I don't?"

"For one thing, I know our nets are about to be overwhelmed with a large catch." Shimon stood and loosened the lines, and motioned for Ari to do the same on his side of the boat. When the nets were secure, he sat down, picked up his oars, and started to row back to shore.

The exertion of rowing against the wind with a full load did not prevent Shimon from talking in a normal voice. "You were orphaned at birth, raised on a kibbutz, and washed out of the army, kidnapped, and taken to Damascus, and later sent to Iran on an undercover mission by the Mossad. Who better to confound the Muslims?" Shimon stared at Ari with a sly grin.

"I don't see the humor," Ari replied, still peeved at such hilarity.

Shimon motioned for Ari to take the second set of oars. "Listen." He paused for dramatic effect. "You will be our Trojan horse."

Ari pulled on his oars with all his strength just to keep up with Shimon's efforts. "You mean I should embrace my role as the Hidden Imam and go along with their program?"

"Play along with them. Find out their game plan. Keep your handler in the Mossad, informed of course." Shimon's face shone with self-congratulation on his analysis of the situation.

Ari relaxed his hold on the oars and sat in stunned silence as Shimon rowed the rest of the way back to shore. The idea of accepting his role as the Mahdi in order to thwart the Brotherhood's plans had never occurred to him. It seemed a preposterous and loathsome proposition. Yet, at the same time, the idea burned deep in his blood. He sat in a trance as he listened intently for something out there in the brooding darkness. Maybe he *could* do what Shimon had suggested. Maybe he *was* chosen for this task. Maybe he *was* in fact the Mahdi. "*Has v'hallilah*, God forbid," he whispered to himself.

Ari coughed to clear his throat. "Just for the sake of argument, suppose I go along with the Mahdi Brotherhood." He carefully chose his words as he continued. "What if I accept the adulation and honor due to this prophet and go over to their side for real?" Ari felt a slight hesitation in the movement of the boat as his partner missed a beat while he thought this over.

Shimon then rowed even harder, pushing the boat through the water with ease. "You do what you have to do, my brother. God has given you free will."

Ari made no response until they approached the shore. "You're saying I have the choice to accept my destiny or not?"

Chapter 1

Ari left at dawn, and kissed his wife and baby daughter goodbye without waking them. He understood his decision the night before had not only bewildered Lily, but had made her angry. Her focus was Abigail, and he didn't flinch when she told him his priorities were out of line. As he walked away from the house, he heard the melancholy sob of the mourning doves that nested under the red roof tiles.

A few short blocks up the main road, Ari bought a ticket at the Tiberias bus station. Though lost in his own thoughts, he still made careful note of a person who boarded the bus minutes later. This man munched on a breakfast bagel like any other local Galilean, but wore the loosely fitted jacket undercover agents wore to conceal a weapon. Ari assumed the Mossad had requested Shin Bet to keep him under surveillance.

Another man boarded the bus and sat in the seat just behind the driver. Ari studied the grease-stained hands and dirty trousers, and concluded he must be a mechanic on his way to work.

The bus pulled out of the station with the motor grumbling as they climbed the steep, curving street which led out of town. Halfway to the top of the plateau, they passed the roadside marker which indicated they had now reached sea level. The bus picked up speed at the top, and then roared across the green countryside, skirting the hills of Nazareth before descending to the Jezreel plain. They pulled into the station in the small town of Hadera, and the passengers who continued on to Tel Aviv remained aboard. Those who had transfers for a Haifa or Jerusalem bus stood around the crowded terminal, and bought freshly roasted nuts or soft drinks.

Ari neither ate nor drank. He assumed the agent assigned to follow him was fresh out of university, as the man went to buy a newspaper and a bottle of water. A more experienced field agent would never have turned his back on his subject.

Ari slept fitfully through the two-hour journey up to Jerusalem, only waking when they pulled into the station. Now hungry and thirsty, he stopped at the first café he saw on Jaffa Road. He took his time savoring the strong, black coffee, then inhaled the crisp air of Jerusalem, so unlike the dense, moist air of Tiberias. For one brief moment, he allowed himself to relax. Then he remembered Lily, and felt remorse for leaving her in such a miserable state of mind.

"Right," he said, as he gulped the rest of his drink. "I'll make it up to her, somehow." He tossed some money on the counter and walked out, squinted in the bright sunlight, and walked toward the Old City situated on the other end of Jaffa Road. A sardonic smile flitted across his lips as he imagined the surprise the Mahdi Brotherhood would experience when he showed up unannounced.

Ari passed the Russian Compound and deliberately did not look at the Mossad headquarters to his left. He turned the corner at the building known as Barclays Bank, crossed a narrow lane, and then entered the open gate of the Saint Louis Hospice. There he stood in the shadow of an archway to detect if anyone tailed him. It did not surprise him to see the young agent from the bus rush past. He immediately recognized the strange, sweet smell of death as he entered the nursing home. To avoid an encounter with the French nuns who tended the dying, he took the stairs down to the kitchen.

"Salaam alechem," Ari mumbled. A startled Arab woman looked up from her chopped vegetables. Before

she had time to respond, he slipped out the back door. He made a full circle around the building, then crossed Paratrooper Boulevard and entered Saint Stephen's Gate. He paused to get his bearings before continuing on the main lane in the *shuk*.

From here it was only a short distance to the watch repair shop in the Muslim Quarter. His brother, Reza, had advised him to go to this place when he wanted to contact the Brotherhood. He knew the risk to approach in broad daylight, but as he had just lost his Mossad tail, he felt secure.

Ari stood for a few minutes and peered through the fly-speckled glass window. A few cheap Timex watches sat on display. He watched the reflection of pedestrians in the dim window, and noted one or two tourists and one old man pushing a cart. He saw nothing to set off his internal alarm.

Just before he pushed open the door, his hand froze in mid-air as he caught a glimpse of the same mechanic who had boarded the bus in Tiberias. Ari slowly exhaled, unable to believe what his eyes told him. Who did this man work for?

Did he imagine a hint of a smile on the mechanic's face? Did he mock him? Ari's heart raced as he crossed the threshold. He shut the door behind him and let his eyes adjust to the dim light. The place smelled musty. It looked like a long-abandoned museum, with dusty display cases on the right, and floor to ceiling shelves on the left. He half expected to see remnants of the Dead Sea scrolls behind the glass, but it turned out to be a motley collection of old clocks.

"Welcome." A short man with a bald head and large, round jowls smiled broadly at him, and then dipped his head in a friendly gesture.

"Fatimah sends her respects," Ari replied. He fervently hoped the secret code had not changed in the years he'd had no contact with the Brotherhood.

"Ali responds in kind." The shopkeeper spoke in a monotone. He then turned and pushed aside a heavy damask curtain revealing an inner chamber.

"I am Abu Rashid. I have been expecting you. Please, come and take some refreshment after your long journey." The shopkeeper approached a side table on which sat a samovar and other utensils for tea making.

Ari had no doubt the mechanic on the bus was a member of the Mahdi Brotherhood. He had been under constant surveillance, and not just by the Mossad. Did Pincus know the Brotherhood had watched his every move?

Abu Rashid motioned for him to take a low stool before a round brass table. He then placed a bowl of nuts and a plate of dates on it. From a small silver tray, he offered a glass of steaming mint tea.

The man obviously had expected him, which meant only one thing. The mechanic must have phoned ahead. Ari drank the tea and politely refused the dates and nuts. He heard the shop door open and a man dressed in a white cloak and a green turban joined them in the inner room. For one terrible moment, Ari believed he was looking into the black, opaque eyes of Abd Umar, the leader of the group in Damascus who, years ago, had orchestrated his kidnapping from Ben Gurion Airport. Despite the cool temperature of the room, sweat beaded on the back of Ari's neck. His muscles tensed as the man in the green turban bowed deeply before him.

Ari forced himself to act the part of the mysterious messiah. He had done this before, and could do it again. He moved his hand in the direction of the other stool, and gave the visitor permission to sit. The shopkeeper brought a glass of tea balanced on the same silver tray and offered it to the man, who accepted and then set it on the table without sipping.

Ari took the man's refusal to drink as a sign of distrust. He would have to win this person's confidence quickly or the meeting would collapse in confusion. Ari had come to Jerusalem to seek answers, but now he realized he must take command, and act the part of the Holy One.

"You are dissatisfied with the refreshment?" Ari's tone sounded deceptively soft.

"No, your Excellency, I am honored to sit before you."

"Then drink." He made it a command not a request.

The man in the green turban took one delicate sip then returned the glass to the table. He then lifted his gaze and stared in awe at Ari.

Ari felt a rush of adrenalin flood his veins. He secretly exalted in this manifestation of raw power. The men in the Mahdi Brotherhood were prepared to execute his orders, satisfy his every wish. Why had he not appreciated this before? He had always felt special, even as a young orphan. Then he'd met Lily at Bet Shalom. She believed in him. She also believed in the supernatural. Who could say he was *not* the Hidden Imam? Was he not born in unusual circumstances during the Six Day War? Did not the lion-shaped scar on his cheek confirm his identity?

He would not impersonate the Mahdi. He *would be* the Mahdi. He, Ari Ben Chaim, held in his hands the destiny not only of Israel, but also all of the Middle East.

Later that day, Ari and the man in the green turban left the Old City, and he made a conscious effort to get his bearings as they drove through Wadi Joz. On the crest of the Mount of Olives, their vehicle sped at reckless speed behind the Church of the Ascension. There he noted a maze of small lanes, wide enough for only one vehicle at a time.

Ari now realized they were on the backside of the Mount of Olives. He had never been there before but recollected from his training in the IDF there were several Arab villages nestled in the hills above the Judean wilderness. In broad daylight, he would expect to catch a glimpse of the Dead Sea in the far distance.

The orange beams from the headlights of the Subaru bounced along the rutted trail which passed for a semblance of a road. The man in the green turban, who called himself Aga Hassan, sat in the front passenger seat. Ari sat behind the driver, the mechanic from the Tiberias bus station. Judging by the way he gunned the engine and drove heedlessly through the dusk, he might very well have been an auto mechanic. No vehicle could take this kind of daily abuse without constant maintenance.

Here and there, a kerosene lamp glimmered behind a curtained window. Strange to think they still did not have electricity in some of the smaller villages. Ari marveled at the Palestinian leadership's continued indifference to basic infrastructure. Surely, the millions donated over the years by the European community had been adequate for the task. He shrugged. There were bigger concerns to deal with just now.

As the designated Holy One, Ari's historic role was to bring peace and tranquility to the earth, starting in Jerusalem, and then spreading to Mecca and on through the entire world. He had no idea how to accomplish this feat. But he knew the Mahdi Brotherhood had infiltrated all segments of society from Tehran to Cairo. Its adherents were even planted in the Vatican and various capitals of Europe.

The noise of the engine slowed and then came to a dead stop. Ari stared out the window at the glow from a gatekeeper's lantern. The driver got out and, with a flourish, opened the car door for him.

The scent of wild sage mingled with goat dung took Ari back to his time spent in Hamed's village south of Bet Lehem. What had happened to Hamed and his family during the intervening years? Then his thoughts turned to Dr. Heftsibah Klein, whom Hamed had worked for all those years before the first intifada.

Ari knew Dr. Klein would disapprove of his decision to take on this role. He valued her opinion but sensed he would never see her again, and therefore it did not matter if he gained her approval or not. He could not turn back now.

"Follow me, your Excellency." The green turban bobbed as Aga Hassan gestured with his hand toward the open gate.

The outward appearance of the compound showed neglect and indifference. Stones in the wall, dislodged by winter storms, lay where they fell. The modest two-story bungalow badly needed a coat of whitewash. The gravel path appeared to have been recently raked, as if in anticipation of this visit. But how did they know? He had made up his mind to visit Jerusalem only last night.

Ari was supposed to be the one prescient, and presumably able to appear and disappear whenever he chose. Did these people have the power to read the future as well?

The front door opened from inside and revealed an entrance hall that, unlike the outside of the building, was not in disrepair. Hand-woven tribal carpets graced the tile floor. The faint scent of cardamom hung delicately in the air. A servant dressed in a simple black robe, showed them where to leave their shoes. Ari and Aga Hassan, but not the driver, were ushered into another room even more opulently furnished.

Ari could never have anticipated that on the backside of the Mount of Olives, in an impoverished village, even by Palestinian standards, a secret house had been carefully prepared for the Holy One. He wondered what Pincus and his colleagues in the Mossad would say if they knew.

Chapter 2

A week passed with no word from Ari, with not a phone call nor a note in the mail. Lily, not the type of woman who waited passively, packed a shoulder bag with a supply of disposable diapers, a few extra t-shirts for the baby and one clean blouse for herself. With Abigail wrapped in the cloth sling close to her chest, she locked the front door to the cottage and headed for the bus station, using the same route Ari had taken seven days earlier.

If Lily worried about being watched, she gave no indication. She felt as calm as possible as she made an uneventful bus journey up to Jerusalem. Upon arrival she went directly to Christ Church Hostel, inside Jaffa Gate, and paid for a night's lodging. After dinner in the refectory, she returned to her room and nursed her daughter while lying on the cool, white sheets. Then she safely bolstered the child with a pillow before falling into a deep slumber.

She awoke early the next morning to the sounds of the Old City's church bells and the high, slightly nasal pitch of the muezzin calling the Muslim faithful to prayer. The baby stirred, and before she could add her cries to the noisy din, Lily breast-fed her. Afterwards, she changed

Abigail's diaper and dressed her in a pink t-shirt that matched her baby bonnet. Lily took a quick shower, slipped on the same denim skirt she'd worn the day before, and then put on a fresh blouse. Holding the baby on her left hip, she went downstairs to find something to eat. On the other side of the cobbled courtyard, she peered into the dining room window, only to see a dark and empty room. Then she noticed the signboard beside the door announced breakfast was served between seven and eight a.m.

"This will never do. I need tea and juice to keep my milk flowing," she said to her daughter, who replied with a soft gurgle. She glanced at her watch, feeling famished and thirsty. Five forty-five. Will the gate be open this early? Glancing across the courtyard to the gate, she smiled in relief to see the gatekeeper shuffling to his post, holding a large ring full of old-fashioned iron keys. She knew Christ Church had been built in the late 1800's, but nevertheless, it amused her that the Church of England, which owned the hostel, had never bothered to modernize with electronic gates.

"*Salaam alechem*, peace to you," the old man said in Arabic. He wore a well-used black suit and a clean white shirt but no tie.

"*Boker tov*, good morning," Lily responded in Hebrew as she approached him.

"You go out early?" He switched to broken English as their common language.

Lily glanced at her child, "I need to find something to eat and drink so I can feed her."

The gatekeeper nodded knowingly. "Too early. Come." He motioned with his head back towards the refectory.

"It's closed. I tried already."

"We go kitchen. My son-in-law cooks."

After a brief introduction to the cook and his assistant, Lily sat at a large wooden table. Soon a bowl of steaming oatmeal appeared before her, along with a pitcher of milk and a glass of orange juice.

Lily thanked her benefactors and dug into the meal, using her right hand while she held Abigail in her left. When the cook's assistant put out her arms to hold baby Abigail, Lily didn't hesitate to hand her over.

By the time the sun rose above the Mount of Olives, Lily was ready to continue her search for Ari. She had no firm plan of action, but it had always been her nature to step out in faith and start walking. God would guide her by circumstances, and if need be, by the intervention of the archangel Michael. Even she admitted angelic intervention happened rarely these days, and only in the most unusual turn of events. Still, she had a history with the archangel that could not be easily dismissed. Michael had directed her to move to Jerusalem, before she ever met Ari. Michael had also told her where to find the burial tomb that contained the petrified almond branch.

Leaving Christ Church, she stood in the main square. She observed the shopkeepers raising the metal doors on storefronts. A cluster of Orthodox Jews, in black coats and fur hats, strolled to the Western Wall for morning prayers. Three border patrol officers headed for the nearby police station, and several Arab workmen made their way to some construction site, judging by the tools they carried.

Lily stood still, breathing in the sweet morning air of Jerusalem. The ancient cobblestones, still slightly damp from the early dew, gave off an earthy scent, like the smell of old cedars and dry riverbeds. She could turn to the left and leave the Old City through Jaffa Gate and walk to the Russian Compound. There she knew she could find agent Pincus, who may or may not have known of Ari's disappearance. Or, she could turn right and take David Street through the market place, and end up near the Temple Mount. While she pondered her choices, she heard a familiar voice call her name.

Professor Scott took off his brown felt hat and raised it straight up so she could see him standing across the square. He had cut his hair short since Lily had seen him last and grown a modest beard. Dressed in khaki slacks and a sport shirt, he looked like the middle-aged archaeologist that he was.

As she approached him, she felt bemused puzzlement. They met in the middle, causing the light vehicle traffic to go around them.

"What a pleasant surprise." Professor Scott put his hat back on his head and warmly shook her hand. "And this is?" He nodded at the baby snuggled in the sling on her chest.

"Abigail, six months old this week." Lily beamed with pride as the professor smiled down on her like a proud uncle. Then she frowned. "What brings you to Jerusalem? I thought you worked in the Galilee."

"That's a long story, but where is the proud father?" He looked around as if expecting Ari to run up and greet him.

"I don't know. That's why I'm here in Jerusalem." She anxiously pushed a loose curl off her forehead.

Professor Scott took her elbow firmly in hand. "Come, we must get out of the middle of the square." He led her toward a café where the proprietor had just placed two tables and four chairs on the patio. "Have you had breakfast?" At her nod he said, "Let's talk over a cup of coffee then."

After they placed their order for one Turkish coffee and one latte, they waited until the server disappeared before resuming their conversation.

"So, what's going on? You two seem to mix with peculiar people," Scott said.

She knew the professor referred to the encounter at Banias where Pincus had whisked them away in a military jeep with an armed escort. She also knew the professor would not forget the dig in Ain Karem where they had recovered a petrified twig from an almond branch and a couple of polished stones.

When their drinks were served, Lily sipped hers thoughtfully. Professor Scott, ignoring his small cup of bitter black coffee, waited for her to speak.

Stalling, Lily asked him where he lodged in Jerusalem. Not that she felt he couldn't be trusted, or that he would laugh in disbelief. On the contrary, she knew he could be depended on to be discreet, still she felt the need to be cautious.

"In answer to your question, I've a dig house over in East Jerusalem. Where are you and baby Abigail staying?"

"We're at the Anglican Hostel right here on the square, at least for the time being. It's reasonably priced and safe."

Scott gazed directly in her eyes. "Is there a need to feel safe?"

Lily bent to kiss the top of Abigail's head.

"Let me phrase it another way. Are you or Ari in some kind of trouble?"

Abigail had by this time fallen asleep. The sweet rosebud lips and thick lashes on her closed eyes made Lily wince with fierce maternal love.

"I'm afraid Ari's gone off the deep end." She paused to gauge Scott's reaction. Seeing no sign of alarm or dismay on his face, she continued. "Remember, back in Ain

Karem, when Ari told you about being mistaken for the Mahdi?"

Scott's face revealed confusion.

"You remember. The Mahdi Brotherhood thinks Ari is the Hidden Imam."

Scott smiled faintly appearing to comprehend.

Lily exhaled heavily. "I thought after Abigail's birth he would put all that behind him and just be a regular husband and father."

Scott picked up his coffee and took a small sip before responding. "You call yourself a regular housewife and mother? You who speak with angels? You who came close to finding the Ark of the Covenant?"

Ignoring the irony in his questions, Lily responded, "Well, not close enough. I didn't find the Ark, did I?"

"No, but you did find a few interesting artifacts. Do you still have those stones? And the twig?"

"Yes, and no, but back to Ari. He's gotten it into his head to play the game their way. He's pretending to be the real Mahdi in order to find out their schemes against Israel."

Scott slowly stroked his beard. "Do you believe he is pretending to be the Mahdi or do you believe he really thinks he is?"

"Who knows?" After a long pause she continued in a barely audible tone, "He's been gone more than a week without contacting me. He wouldn't do that if not under some kind of restraint."

"I see." Scott's demeanor softened as he recalled how devoted Ari had always been. "How can I help you?"

Lily shrugged one shoulder. "It was no accident we met here this morning."

Scott lowered his voice. "I believe it's no accident someone is watching us."

Lily casually glanced over at the next table. She observed a young man drinking coffee. He wore jeans and a loose shirt. She hadn't noticed him before due to her intensive conversation with Scott. But now she suspected that Shin Bet had her under surveillance, most likely since she left Tiberias. But if Pincus ordered surveillance on her then they surely had also followed Ari.

"I know what to do. Watch me," Lily said in a low voice.

Chapter 3

Lily saw a look of puzzlement cross Scott's face as she nestled the baby close to her chest, and walked over to the seated secret agent. "I need to talk with Motti Pincus. Now," she said to the startled Israeli.

The young man responded by punching numbers on his cell phone. He spoke in the rapid Hebrew of a Sabra, which Lily barely managed to follow. Then he glanced furtively at her and said, "Sit down. He will be here in five minutes. Your friend over there should join us."

Lily recognized a command, not a request, and waved Scott to their table. He promptly responded.

At that moment, the Arab waiter approached Lily. "You know this man?" He glanced nervously in the direction of the Israeli.

"What do you think?" Lily's curt tone caused the waiter to turn and make a rapid retreat to the kitchen area. "I guess he recognizes a Shin Bet agent when he sees one." She gave a mirthless smile.

An awkward silence prevailed. Finally, Lily broke the impasse by attempting an introduction. "Professor Eugene Scott." She used his full title, even though he had moments before asked her to call him simply Scott. "Let me introduce you." Here she paused for effect. "What is your name?" She asked the agent.

"You can call me Benny." He raised his gaze and locked eyes with Scott but made no attempt to shake hands.

"Well," Scott said, "what a day of coincidences. First Lily runs into one old friend and then another."

Lily suppressed a laugh. "Benny is not my friend."

Scott pulled a pipe out of his pocket and proceeded to fill it with sweet-smelling tobacco from a leather pouch.

"And what's your line of work?" He stared intently at the young man.

"Security," the Israeli replied bluntly. "And yourself?"

"I'm here to gather pollen samples from a recently unearthed cistern in the City of David." Scott struck a match and concentrated on lighting his pipe.

The agent narrowed his eyes as he measured the man sitting across the small table. "Who is the lead investigator on your dig?"

"Professor Evron of Haifa University, you know him?"

"I've heard of him. I just wanted to know if you were an amateur or the real thing. All sorts of people come to Israel pretending to be archaeologists." Benny snorted in disapproval.

Without announcement, a third gentleman quietly sat down with them. Tall and thin, with pale slightly freckled skin, he wore a dress shirt with the sleeves rolled up and no tie.

"Lily, how good to see you again, and your little one as well." The newcomer's gaze rested on the sleeping baby in her lap. "And who is your friend? Haven't we met before?"

A look of puzzlement flickered in Scott's eyes. Then after a long, awkward pause, he replied, "I believe we ran into each other near Tel Dan some time ago. As I recall, Lily had unexpectedly fainted, and you just happened to be there with an army jeep and carried her away."

Recognition flashed on the countenance of the Mossad agent. He nodded in agreement.

Lily looked first at Pincus than at Scott. Did it matter where they had run into each other? The important issue was Ari. She closed her eyes in irritation and frowned.

As if Pincus could read her mind, he turned back to her. "Where is your husband this fine morning?"

Her muscles tensed. If Pincus asked an honest question, not a rhetorical one, the Mossad and their partners in Shin Bet had lost Ari's trail. With a sinking feeling, she assumed Ari must have crossed over to the other side. Her intuition now told her not only a physical distance but also an ideological chasm separated her from her husband. Had the mystique of the Hidden Mahdi overtaken him? If so, she could do nothing. She visibly shivered, detecting evil in the very air she breathed.

Like a small animal picks up the scent of fear in its mother, Abigail stirred in her arms. Lily leaned over to whisper gentle shushing sounds to reassure her. At the same time, she let her auburn hair fall across her face to hide her distress from the three men now staring at her. It was imperative she hide this newly found insight from Pincus. He wouldn't understand. In fact, he would call Ari a *boded*, a traitor to the State of Israel.

Lily didn't have a word to describe her husband, but she knew it would not be traitor. An element of mystery in all this remained, and she could not decipher it. But she knew Ari to be a good man, who would never bring harm to his family, or to his country.

She slowly raised her eyes and looked straight ahead, staring at the stone fortress across the square. She knew this structure was called David's Citadel, although in fact it had been built many centuries after the time of King David. But she also knew people liked to believe anything expedient or popular.

And so, Lily made the decision to tell agent Pincus what she thought he wanted to hear. Not the truth. He certainly didn't need to know Ari had emotionally and physically crossed the invisible frontier that separated Jews and Muslims. She was painfully aware both groups looked to the same ancestor, Abraham, but from there their paths diverged. The Jewish scriptures told of Isaac being the legal heir. The Muslim scriptures called Ishmael the true heir. Having both strains running through his DNA, she knew Ari had the option of choosing one or the other, and he had evidently chosen to follow the lineage of Ishmael, culminating in the return of the Twelfth Imam.

Lily felt the tension build around her while she made her decision to trust Scott but not Pincus. Scott had no ulterior motives. Their paths crossed this morning, but only by chance. On the other hand, Pincus kept a surveillance team on her, not because he cared about her welfare, but as a matter of national security.

Having made her decision, she looked at Pincus without blinking and told him a falsehood. "Ari's gone into the desert for a time of meditation. He will return and join Abigail and me at the Anglican Hostel in a few days."

Without missing a beat, Pincus asked, "The Judean wilderness or the Negev?"

"Somewhere near Ein Gedi, beyond the waterfalls," Lily replied with false certitude.

Pincus stood and then bowed to Lily in an old-fashioned mode as he took his leave. Whether he believed her or not, Lily knew he was too much a professional to reveal it.

The younger agent, not able to cloak his thoughts, awkwardly tossed some shekels on the table with an expression of doubt in the angle of his jaw.

After they left, Scott took out a cotton handkerchief and mopped his brow. "Do you want to explain any of this?"

"As I said earlier, I need your help. Ari has gone over to the other side." Lily whispered calmly, as if meeting with a Mossad agent was an everyday event in her life.

"Then he is not camping somewhere in the Judean wilderness?"

"He might be. I know he's where I can't reach him."

"Reach him physically, or spiritually?"

Lily stared at Scott, impressed with his discernment. "I suppose I mean both. I don't know where he is geographically. But I have some idea of where he is in the spiritual sense." She paused and looked around the restaurant patio to make sure no waiter or patron stood within hearing distance.

She continued in a low whisper, "Ari has a peculiar background, as you already know. The Mahdi Brotherhood believes he is the long-awaited Twelfth Imam. All kinds of signs supposedly confirm this."

"Refresh my memory." Scott puffed harder on his pipe as if to draw sustenance from the nicotine.

"You know of his birth during the Six Day War, the lion-shaped scar on his cheek, his mixed bloodlines, both Jewish, and Iranian."

"I thought he didn't believe any of it." Scott's voice sounded dry and matter-of-fact.

"That's just it. He always thought these men from the Brotherhood were delusional. Then he came home one evening and announced he had to fulfill his destiny. He left the next day for Jerusalem. After some time passed with no word from Ari, I packed up Abigail and came here to search for him."

Scott laid down his pipe and pointedly asked, "Why is the Mossad involved?"

Lily brusquely smoothed her hair back from her face. "The Mossad sent Ari undercover to Iran several years ago. They just like to keep tabs on their operatives, current or retired."

"Is he retired?" Scott's eyes never left her face.

"Oh yeah, he has no connection with them. This much I know."

"But he has maintained his connections to this Brotherhood?"

"That's just it. He received a cryptic email message from his half-brother, Reza, and it so upset him he dismantled his computer. I thought he'd finished with all this Mahdi business." She sniffled, holding back her tears.

Scott stood and extended his hand to assist Lily to her feet. "Let's take a walk about the Old City. The brisk morning air will do us good, plus I have something special to show you."

Chapter 4

"I want to show you something I've recently discovered near the City of David," Scott said looking at his watch. "It will take about an hour."

Lily felt a thrill of anticipation at the mention of this ancient settlement. *If only Ari were here. He would be interested in any new find that pertained to King David.*

Lily checked the baby's diaper. "Before we traipse around, I need to change Abigail. Wait here."

She started to walk toward the hostel, then turned back and whispered to Scott, "Use this time to see if anyone is shadowing us."

"What do you mean?"

"Be alert, and watch who comes and goes on the street."

Lily returned ten minutes later with a contented baby vigorously sucking on a pacifier. She found Scott leaning casually against the outside wall of the hostel compound.

"See anything suspicious?"

Scott answered, "Just the usual mix of people I would expect to see in this place, an Armenian priest, tourists, one motorcycle and a car or two."

The roar of an approaching motorcycle made them jump back out of the narrow roadway. A helmeted driver on a small red Suzuki sped by raising a mini dust storm on the cobblestones.

"That fool shouldn't be allowed on the public roads. It's the second time I've seen him." Scott scowled.

Lily frowned. "That's what I meant by keeping alert. If you've seen him twice, he's probably tailing us. I'll bet he rushed ahead to wait for us down the road. He didn't know I'd stop for a diaper change."

Scott hesitated then abruptly turned and motioned for Lily to follow him. He passed one shop and turned into a lane wide enough only for pedestrians. "Even a motorcycle can't negotiate the twists and turns in the Armenian Quarter."

Taking long strides to keep up, Lily scanned the narrow alley and realized she'd been there before. She looked up and recognized the window in the middle of a stone archway. "Dan and Eli live here," she called out to Scott who walked a few paces ahead.

Scott slowed down and turned to face Lily. "Who?"

"Old friends from Rosh Pinna."

"Friends like Pincus, the spymaster?"

"Totally different." Lily looked wistfully up at the window as she recalled happier times.

Scott turned and continued down the lane with Lily and the baby following in his wake. They maneuvered through the Armenian neighborhood without further incident, arriving at the ancient Roman market place, the Cardo, now renovated and lined with upscale designer boutiques. Crossing the Roman road, they entered the parking square of the rebuilt Jewish Quarter.

"Wait up," Lily called to Scott. "I need to tighten the baby's sling." As she pulled the length of cloth tighter around her shoulder and under her arm, she sniffed the top of Abigail's head, now slightly damp with the sweet perfume of infant perspiration. "You're such a comfort to me," she murmured in Abigail's ear.

"Need some help?" Scott stopped and waited for her to catch up. "I could carry her."

Lily shook her head. "We're fine, lead on."

"Do you still think we're being followed?"

"I'm not sure." Lily squared her shoulders as much as she could under the weight of the child and indicated with a lift of her chin she was ready to continue. "How much farther?"

"We're close to the Dung Gate. What I want to show you is not far outside the wall. It's just before the City of David on the other side of the Kidron Valley."

They soon joined the ranks of Hassidic Jews, pilgrims, and the occasional band of tourists converging on the plaza in front of the Western Wall. Going through the security checkpoint without incident, they skirted the center of the plaza. They gave a wide berth to the table where the kippot for men's heads and the scarves for women with sleeveless dresses were handed out to anyone foolish enough to have arrived at this outer wall of the temple without adequate covering.

Scott nodded a friendly greeting to the Border Patrol officers on duty as they exited at the Dung Gate, but they barely acknowledged him. The crowds entering the gate fully occupied their attention as they searched for weapons or explosives.

"You remember my field of expertise is the First Century Roman era." Scott led her along the road which bordered the Kidron Valley.

Lily nodded, though in fact she had forgotten this detail. Most people were more interested in the Iron Age discoveries. "Does anyone care about the Roman period?"

Scott stopped to look at her. "Are you serious? Pax Romana ruled the known world. It's like asking how relevant the United States was in the Twentieth Century." He shook his head and chuckled at the look of doubt on her face. "Although the Jews like to ignore the fact, this is the period when Jesus of Nazareth walked this land."

A broad smile crossed Lily's face. "I don't ignore the history of Jesus. My friends who live back there in the Armenian quarter are Jews who follow the teachings of Yeshua Ha Mashiach."

Scott paused. "What I'm about to show you is in a different category, or the opposite side of the coin, so to speak."

"Quit talking in riddles. What have you found?"

"Who was Christ's greatest adversary?" Scott's expression revealed barely suppressed glee.

"I don't know, maybe Judas?"

"No, someone before him."

Lily shifted the baby's weight and patted her plump cheek. "I give up. Tell me."

"Lucifer, the fallen angel." A note of triumph sounded in the professor's voice as he pointed across the Kidron Valley. "There, behind that smaller monument on the left. See it? Just above Absalom's monument. I've found evidence of an ancient altar used by a Luciferian cult."

Lily turned her gaze to follow his hand. At the same time, she suddenly felt queasy in the pit of her stomach.

"Come, I'll show you." Scott started down the incline following a seldom-used path. After a few paces, he turned to Lily. "Need some help?"

"I don't feel well." Lily walked with hesitant steps, searching the path for loose pebbles.

"What's wrong?" Scott reached out his hand for her to grasp.

"Do you believe in premonitions?" Lily tightly held on to him.

"Not really, but you look frightened. What scared you?"

"A morbid sense of doom hovers in this valley."

"Let's continue on a little way and then see how you feel."

At the bottom of the incline, they stopped to rest beside the dry stream. Scott stooped down to examine what looked like stunted weeds growing between the dusty rocks.

"No! I can't cross the water." Lily cried out.

Scott looked up in surprise. "What?"

"The rushing water is black and oily. We'll drown if we cross it." Trembling uncontrollably, Lily stepped back.

Scott stared in disbelief at Lily then at the dry creek. "There's no water."

"Can't you smell the putrid sulfur fumes?" Lily backed away from Scott.

Puzzled, the professor tried to assess the situation. "I don't smell anything, but I see you're spooked by something here."

"There." Lily pointed to the area above Absolom's Tomb on the other side of the *wadi*. "Do you see the dark shadow moving among the ruins?"

Scott put his hand above his eyes to block the glare from the sun. He looked steadily for several moments. "I don't see anything, but I believe you do. Let's turn around and go back."

Even as he spoke, Lily started back up the trail at a quicker pace than she had descended. At the summit, she stopped to catch her breath. Instinctively she hid Abigail's face under her outer clothing.

"What frightened you down there?"

"An evil-smelling river rushed through the *wadi*. The black, oily water would kill us if we tried to cross it. And then I saw a shadowy figure creeping among the tombs." She could see she had not convinced the professor. "Could it have been some sort of manifestation of Lucifer?"

Scott fumbled around in his pockets for his pipe, stalling for time. He replied in a calm voice, "I understand you communicate with the archangel Michael. I remember that from my stay in Ain Karem." He motioned for Lily to sit on a large, flat boulder by the side of the road while he filled his pipe and lit a match. "By the way, you're probably sitting on a first-century stone carved for the temple."

"Don't change the subject, professor. I sensed evil down there in the streambed. Rationally, I know there was no water, black or oily. All I know is I couldn't go any further. I'll leave the findings of cultic worship to you, if you don't mind. Abigail and I want to go back to our room."

"Right you are." Scott grasped Lily's hand and helped her up. "Can she breathe in there?" He peered nervously at the baby carrier.

"I can feel every breath she takes." Lily patted Abigail's backside to reassure him. "Now let's return the quickest way."

Back in the safety and comfort of her room, Lily put Abigail down for a nap and stretched out on the bed beside her. Suffering from a raging headache, she closed her eyes and sought oblivion in sleep. Sleep came, but not tranquility. In her dreams, angels faced each other in blazing flashes of light and thunder. Michael pitted against Lucifer. Lily moaned softly in her sleep and placed a protective hand over the child lying next to her.

Chapter 5

The following morning, Lily woke to the reassuring sound of chirping birds, and after the harrowing events of the previous day, any bit of normalcy felt comforting. Abigail stirred in her nest of blankets like the baby birds outside the window. She would soon be demanding food. Lily splashed cool water on her face and then drank from the flask on the bedside table. The pleasant sensation of her milk letting down coincided with the first plaintive wail.

An hour later, dressed and ready to face the day, Lily positioned the baby in her sling and stepped out into the courtyard. The oppressive events of the day before lay heavily on her mind, but determined to face the new morning with optimism, she focused on the birds flitting in and out from the eaves. To pass the time until the dining room opened, and out of curiosity, she pushed on the heavy wooden door of the Anglican Church and entered the foyer. Light from the tall, narrow windows fell on her as she walked down the main aisle of the sanctuary. The not unpleasant scent reminded her of a musty library.

She sat on a hard wooden pew and stared at the stained glass windows as the sunlight created a rainbow pattern across the stonework. To her surprise, a feeling of peace and tranquility enveloped her, the opposite of the sensation she had experienced yesterday in the Kidron Valley. "What's happening to me?" she murmured to Abigail, who noisily sucked on her pacifier. "Yesterday I almost lost it."

When the bell rang announcing breakfast, she left the church, grateful for the distraction. The hostel manager, a tall Englishman with gray hair and a mustache, strode toward her as she approached the dining room entrance. "Good morning, Mrs. Ben Chaim. I see you've just come from our sanctuary."

"Yes," Lily replied. "I hope I wasn't intruding." Her voice trailed off in a tone of apology.

"Not at all, everyone is welcome." He paused to let her enter the dining room first. "I thought you might be interested to know there's a Shabbat service in Hebrew today."

Lily turned to face him. "In Hebrew? In an Anglican Church?"

"First, why don't you sit down?" He motioned to a table by the window. "May I join you for breakfast as I explain?" Lily nodded as she made herself comfortable, loosening the baby from her sling to position her on her lap.

"In answer to your question, we have services in Russian, Filipino, Hebrew, and English, of course."

"I've never gone to a church service before." Lily held up her cup as the waiter poured the coffee.

The manager continued, "Two Jewish brothers are the pastors of the Hebrew congregation here. Dan and Eli."

Lily nearly choked on her coffee. "I know them. They live nearby, right?"

He looked at her with a pleased expression. "Yes, they do. Why don't you attend service this afternoon? Five o'clock."

Lily spent a quiet day never leaving the church compound, all the time thinking about the two brothers. They had made a big impact on Ari back in Rosh Pinna, where they had first met the pair. Their faith in the Messiah, *Yeshua*, touched something deep in Ari's soul, and yet he seemed to hold back. Therefore, she'd held back. Even now, though her heart wanted to be a part of their world, she knew she could not do so without Ari.

Just before sunset, Lily slipped unnoticed into a back pew. The small gathering of people sang songs in Hebrew, accompanied by a man playing a guitar. Dan gave a message, and afterward there were prayers for the sick. Then it ended. Lily was now proficient enough in Hebrew that she understood almost everything, although she wasn't familiar with some words, apparently theological in content. After the service, she followed the small crowd as they gathered in a side room for refreshments.

Lily approached the brothers standing by the tea table. They looked much the same as she remembered them. Dan, the younger of the two, still had a mop of curly hair and wore the same affable expression on his face. He stood a few inches taller than his brother. Eli was stocky, with straight hair, and wore his usual inscrutable expression.

"Remember me?" She smiled at the astonished expression on their faces.

"Of course, we remember you. But where's Ari? And who is this?" Dan smiled at the baby.

"This is Abigail." Then after an awkward silence, Lily continued. "I don't know where Ari is. He's disappeared."

Eli looked at his brother with concern. "What do you mean Ari's gone? He hasn't left you, has he?"

Lily winced but managed a small laugh. "No, of course not, at least not in the way you're thinking." She could see the relief in their eyes. "His absence has to do with the Mahdi Brotherhood." Now, she saw not just concern but something more ominous in their eyes as they looked at one another.

Dan turned to the handful of people still lingering after the service. "Let me say good night to these people, and then we can talk in private."

Later, Lily and the brothers walked across the courtyard to an old-fashioned sitting area, available to the hostel guests. The spacious, vaulted room looked gloomy and empty, as it usually was on Saturday evening. Lily made herself comfortable on the sofa while Dan and Eli sat opposite her in straight-backed chairs.

"Now, tell us what this is all about," Dan said, always the more direct of the siblings. Lily didn't reply but fussed about and settled the baby, as if stalling for time.

Eli leaned forward with his hands on his knees. "Tell us, what does Ari's disappearance have to do with this Mahdi business?" He looked intently into Lily's eyes. "When we last saw the two of you, we thought you had sorted it out and were finished with those people."

Lily directed her gaze to her lap to hide her discomfort. "I thought the same. Since Abigail's birth, I expected us to live like any other couple. We rented a pleasant cottage in Tiberias." Now she looked across the room as the awkward silence hung in the air.

After some moments, Dan said with gentle insistence, "But?"

"But what?" Lily knew she sounded defensive.

"There is always a 'but' in every dilemma," Eli quietly added. "Did Ari want to call it quits with the Mahdi Brotherhood, but something compelled him to continue the relationship?"

"Something like that." Lily smiled despite herself. Eli's intuitive grasp of the complex situation strangely comforted her.

Eli folded his hands in his lap as if he might start praying. "I have never forgotten the unique circumstance of Ari's birth. As a matter of fact, he's been much on my mind in recent days."

Lily shifted her position on the sofa so Abigail could kick her legs freely. "What's so special about Ari's birth? Infants are abandoned every day all over the world."

"This may be true elsewhere, but not in Israel. Neither Muslims nor Jews abandon a healthy baby boy. How many babies were born and thrown away during the Six Day War? I would guess only one, Ari." Eli paused to let his statement sink in.

"Then, what's so special about the Six Day War?" Lily looked to one then the other.

"It's a long story," Dan began. "But to get to the heart of it, not so many months ago, we met a pastor here in Jerusalem. He lives on Mount Scopus and spends much of his time in prayer. He told us about a vision he had many years ago. He saw a great gathering of angels with their faces turned toward earth. They were eagerly following events taking place on the planet, and obviously desired to participate. But a golden cord held them back in heaven."

Eli picked up the story. "Sometime later, he had a similar vision of angels in heaven, and with the same golden cord holding them back. Only this time the golden cord was drawn aside. Immediately, and with obvious joy, the angels descended to earth. Then the vision ended."

What does this vision have to do with Ari?" Lily held her head to one side in puzzlement.

"Well, the pastor later realized he received this second vision on the first day of the Six Day War. He understood from biblical prophecy that the Six Day War was a decisive turning point in human history, with the restoration of Jerusalem to Jewish control after nearly two thousand years. That explains the excitement and participation of the angels."

"But I still don't see how this involves Ari just because he happened to be born then." Lily defiantly crossed her arms over her chest.

Not fazed by Lily's attitude, Eli replied, "Satan realizes his kingdom is being threatened like never before and is fighting back with every tactic and method he can muster.

Ari, as the so-called Holy One, is being used as a tool of the devil."

"My husband is not a tool of the devil." Lily picked up her restless baby and prepared to leave the room.

Dan quickly countered, "We know he's not. We always said you two were part of the band which would restore the fallen tabernacle of David. Don't you remember?"

"That was long ago. A lot has happened since." Lily tried not to appear offended as she wrapped Abigail in the shoulder sling. "But I need time to think about all this."

The brothers followed Lily out to the courtyard. She started up the stairs and turned to watch the two enter the now-deserted sanctuary before she returned to her room.

Chapter 6

The waves crashed in endless succession on the white sand. The scorching sun at midday kept most of the guests in their cottages or villas reclining on couches and sipping fruit drinks. One or two sturdier souls sat outside on sheltered balconies in the numerous high-rise hotels which broke the skyline on Kish Island.

The vacation getaway of wealthy Iranians, Kish Island on the Persian Gulf was only two hours by air from Tehran, but light years away from the oppressive regime of the ayatollahs and their Revolutionary Guard. If Reza cared to, which he most emphatically did not, he could body surf, snorkel, or swim with dolphins. Entire mornings could be enjoyed on the tennis courts or bicycling. The hotel served delicious cuisine, both European and Persian. Waiters in crisp white jackets served the guests, eager to fulfill their every whim. Live music could be enjoyed every night even though there were no bars or discos.

But the solitary man renting the villa behind the pools and tennis courts led the life of an ascetic. Every morning, Reza received a covered tray with a pot of tea, a bit of goat cheese, and *nan*, the flat bread of the peasants. He never touched the small pot of honey the waiter always added. Then, for his main meal of the day, he requested *abgoosht*, a simple lentil and lamb stew, or *ghormeh sabzi,* a dish of stewed herbs served over rice, the mainstay of the common people of Iran. In the evening, he ate a bowl of yoghurt and more of the flat bread. The rich sauces served in the dining room never tempted his palate, though in his youth, he had delighted to eat the dishes his mother made, like wild duck and crushed walnuts stewed in pomegranate juice. But now, as a senior member of the Mahdi

Brotherhood, indulgence of the bodily appetites must not be encouraged.

The waiters and cleaning staff laughed behind his back at his simple tastes, but at the same time marveled at the rich man who displayed such discipline. Early in the morning, before the heat of the sun began to wilt the potted flowers, he could be observed walking beside the breaking waves. Always alone, he was never seen with a companion. But today would be different. Today he expected a visitor.

All the staff, from the lowliest cleaner, to the concierge in the lobby, stood on alert. A high-ranking cleric from the holy city of Mecca would stay the night. Female guests, intuitively sensing the arrival of an important visitor, wore long-sleeved tunics and pulled silk scarves low over their elaborate hairdos. The air in the hotel crackled with tension, but the rich and powerful knew they were on a relatively safe playing field because Kish Island remained off-limits to the strict enforcement of Islamic jurisprudence. Nevertheless, when the white-bearded cleric arrived and strolled around the grounds deep in conversation with Reza, the guests and even the employees prudently stayed out of sight.

The following morning, the auspicious visitor and his entourage left the hotel in a parade of silver Mercedes. Reza stayed in his room, drinking only the tea, sending the bread and goat cheese back to the kitchen.

It was not illness which caused him to fast this morning, but rather an upset stomach resulting from the tension brought on by the visit of the high-ranking cleric. Reza knew about the enmity between the Shi'ite ayatollahs who ruled from the holy city of Qom in Iran and the Sunni clerics who ruled from the holy city of Mecca. He feared them equally. Both sides of this equation were bringing ruin upon the Middle East.

Reza had no doubt his visitor, dressed so elegantly in his fawn-colored robes, and came to Kish Island for one thing only. He wanted to know when to expect the arrival of the Mahdi.

The white-bearded cleric had whispered, his words dripping like melted butter on his tongue, "We in Mecca should be the first to reveal the Hidden Imam."

Reza had nodded his head in agreement. He readily acknowledged the ayatollahs ruling Iran were out of control, bordering on megalomania. In this he did not perjure himself. He wholeheartedly agreed on this point. However, his face and tone of voice did not reveal that he thought exactly the same about the ruling clique in Mecca.

Years of dissembling had perfected Reza's ability to fool even the most cunning of opponents, and now he had successfully convinced his visitor he was not in a position to contact the Mahdi. "No one knows his exact whereabouts. I do not need to tell you, a learned scholar of the Koran that the Holy One can appear and disappear at will."

At that juncture, with the air bristling with barely concealed hostility, the haughty cleric abruptly strode out of the room and returned to his suite.

The next morning, after the departure of his guest in a roar of expensive vehicles, Reza sighed with deep relief. Now he knew for a certainty Ari had received his message. Otherwise, there would have been no visitor from Mecca. For just as Reza had anticipated they would do, the Mossad monitored all communications to and from the State of Israel. Their friends and close allies in the CIA had been duly informed of such a message. In time, the information had reached the State Department where the Sunni had their own spies. And so the circle closed.

Chapter 7

Still hidden in the secret house on the backside of the Mount of Olives, Ari assumed an imperial manner as he enjoyed special meals each evening. He ordered Devonshire cream, the best Argentine beef, and exotic fruits from all over the world. He requested Danish pastry, and the next day he ate delicious rolls flown in from Copenhagen. This confirmed what he already suspected—the Mahdi network was extensive and well financed.

One day, after breakfast, a servant bowed respectfully. "Aga Hassan would like an audience this morning, if it suits your Excellency." Ari nodded in consent as the servant cleared the low table and hurried out.

Some minutes later Aga Hassan entered the room wearing black clerical robes and the traditional green turban that signified a direct descendent of the Prophet Mohammed. He waited for Ari to give him permission to sit and then moved in a deliberately slow manner, arranging his robes and carefully placing his feet to one side.

"Welcome and peace upon you," Ari said, and then added the usual polite talk about the weather and his visitor's health.

"Your Holiness, if I speak frankly it is only for your well-being and security." Aga Hassan compulsively fingered the prayer beads in his hand.

Ari tried to read the man's countenance. It had been a long time since he had assumed the personage of the Hidden Imam, and he had only recently acquired the subtle expressions of subterfuge any good Muslim learned at his mother's knee.

Ari cautiously smiled at his visitor. "Speak freely, Aga Hassan."

"As you know, this safe haven," Hassan lifted his eyes to take in the opulently furnished room, "has been in existence for many years awaiting your presence."

"But?" Ari prodded gently.

"Since your arrival, I have noticed a flurry of activity around this house, and it has come to my attention a certain person in the village has given information about this location to the Jews."

"And what do you intend to do about this informer?" Ari asked, knowing full well the suspected collaborator was already a dead man.

"The matter is taken care of, but there will be others. Our desire is to ensure your comfort and safety." After a long silence Aga Hassan continued in a whisper. "It is time for you to leave here. I have received word your brother, Reza, is waiting for you in the desert."

Ari controlled his facial expression even as his inner thoughts churned with emotion. This must be the real reason for the visit, not to tell him about an informer. Why did his half-brother want to see him now? Something important was about to take place. Otherwise Reza would not take the risk of exposure.

"Where is he?"

"Jabel Musa."

"Then make the necessary travel arrangements today." With a curt nod, Ari indicated the audience was over. As Aga Hassan slipped out of the room, Ari folded his hands in his lap. "Like Moses, I will find my true calling in the Sinai." He smiled with satisfaction.

* * * *

The black Mercedes sedan pulled away from the secret house before dawn. The driver never spoke a word to Ari in the back seat, dressed in a white linen robe and a green turban. As he had suspected, Aga Hassan did not accompany him on this journey into the desert. Instead, a middle-aged man dressed in a business suit, and carrying a large briefcase, sat next to the driver.

As the sun came up over Moab on the east bank of the Jordan River, the car sped through isolated villages. The driver skillfully chose back roads that bypassed army check points. Traveling southward, they skirted Bet Lehem, and then Hebron, arriving on the edges of the Sinai before noon in the one-hundred plus degree heat.

Ari admired the skill of his driver as he managed to avoid not only the Israeli Army, but also the Egyptian Army as they entered the Sinai. He obviously knew the territory as they drove on dirt roads that had once been camel trails. By evening they reached the plateau below Mount Sinai. The sun set rapidly in the west as the shadows fell like purple curtains. The steep, rugged slopes of Jabel Musa rose as a backdrop. Looking through the tinted windows, Ari could see the black goat-hair tents used by the Bedouin. The driver and his companion in the business suit conferred together in Arabic and then turned to him.

"Your holiness, we will accept the hospitality of our driver's kin. You will eat a meal here and sleep for a few hours before another emissary comes to take you to your final destination."

Ari nodded in approval. It would be good to stretch his legs and flex his shoulders after the long drive.

Stepping out of the Mercedes, he inhaled the savory scent of sage mixed with the sharp smell of dried camel dung burning on open fires. The intense heat of the day had given way to the refreshing chill of the high desert after sundown.

His driver led him to one of the larger tents. Inside, he sat on a woven carpet as a Bedouin brought him a minute cup of black, bitter coffee. The hot liquid burned his throat, and then the caffeine quickened his pulse in a pleasant way. No one seemed inclined to talk, and it suited him perfectly. He'd taken a long journey, and he was tired of keeping up the appearance of being the Holy One. After the coffee came a tin platter which held a dish of goat cheese, freshly baked flat bread, and plump dates.

Surprised at his appetite under the circumstances, Ari ate the plain fare of the desert with enthusiasm, finding it tastier than the rich delicacies he had insisted on in Jerusalem. For the sake of propriety, he left half the dates, not wanting to appear greedy.

By mid-evening, the stars lit up the dome of the sky with such intensity Ari could see the dim outline of the nearby Greek Orthodox monastery known as Santa Catarina on the slope of Mount Sinai. What would he encounter there? *What news did Reza bring that compelled him to arrange this meeting?*

Later, Ari lay on the rough, camel hair carpet with his head resting on his jacket. Hearing an infant cry in a nearby tent, his thoughts turned to Lily, and he wondered what she and baby Abigail were doing this evening. He missed them intensely, even as he forced himself to think of what the morning would bring. There would be time later to figure out how his family fit into his role as the Muslim messiah. He reminded himself that even Mohammed had managed to incorporate his first wife Khadija, and then numerous concubines, into his vision for the spread of Islam.

Ari remembered how it was when he first met the Mahdi Brotherhood in Damascus and later in Iran. At that time, he knew himself to be an imposter and feared for his life. Now, he felt confident in his role and relished the power he held over others, including his half-brother. As he fell asleep in the rough desert tent, he had strange dreams about the Jew from Nazareth, also called a messiah.

At first light, Ari's traveling companion stood outside the tent and coughed discreetly. "I've brought water and your prayer rug."

After ritually washing Ari made his morning prayers in the manner taught to him in Damascus. Then, he drank a cup of steaming hot Arabic coffee alone in his tent.

Later, the Bedouin driver stood at the entrance. "I will take you to the monastery when you are ready."

Driving across the desert, Ari leaned forward to get a better look as the Mercedes approached what looked like a medieval fortress. The high walls surrounding the monastery dwarfed the small entrance gate. A group of tourists stood around the gate of Santa Catarina, apparently waiting for access. Ari's driver parked near the gate, and a bearded young man in the robes of a Greek Orthodox monk approached the Mercedes.

"Welcome," the monk said in English without a trace of an accent. "Follow me."

Ari exited the vehicle, wondering if the young man knew whom he had invited into the compound. He had always wanted to visit the Sinai, but after it returned to Egyptian control in the 1980's, it had been out of bounds for Israeli citizens.

The first thing that caught his eye inside the fortress was the church built by the monks in the sixth century. He noted other smaller buildings, including a library, and what looked like a dormitory. He'd heard tales of a charnel house, which held the skulls of all those who had lived and died here at Santa Catarina throughout the centuries. He did not expect to see a small mosque in the compound. While he stood there, his brother Reza strode out of the mosque and approached with a broad smile on his face.

"Peace to you." Reza embraced Ari and formally kissed him on both cheeks.

"And peace to you," Ari replied, anxious but pleased to see his brother again. Reza had not changed much over the past few years. His hair looked thick and full, though somewhat greyer. He wore a plain linen suit, expertly tailored, and as always, fine Italian loafers.

Reza stood back and motioned for Ari to enter the mosque. "Come inside where we can talk privately." They both removed their shoes at the door.

The interior of the dome-shaped room felt pleasantly cool. The whitewashed walls reflected the light from small windows at the top. The floor was covered with layer after layer of fine carpets. A water pipe stood on the floor near several large, flat cushions. Ari sat on one of them and nodded to Reza to follow suit.

When they were settled, Ari broke the silence. "Well, my brother, I know how the Egyptians fear and hate the Mahdi Brotherhood. What is so urgent you would risk traveling through Cairo, crossing the Red Sea, and driving through the Sinai just to see me?"

Reza laughed softly. "My dear brother, you have the abrupt manners of the Jews who raised you. You always get straight to the point."

Ari shrugged one shoulder in response and smiled to show he took no offense at Reza's critical comment. "I know. First I must ask about your journey, and if all is well with you."

"I am well, Allah be praised," Reza responded. "I bring you greetings from our sister, Ferideh."

"Our sister is in good health and happy in Paris?"

"She is well."

Ari slowly exhaled, knowing Reza would eventually get around to the urgent matter which brought them to the backside of the desert. He was confident the matter would be revealed before the day ended. To make polite conversation, and also to satisfy his curiosity, he decided to ask Reza another question.

"Tell me, my esteemed older brother, how does there happen to be a mosque here?"

Reza's eyebrows lifted slightly, as if to indicate Ari should already know the answer to such a question. "Ah, now you are testing me again." Reza looked at his hands and folded them in his lap. "Tradition says in the seventh century, Mohammed took refuge in the Sinai and had an encounter with the monks here. Afterward, he issued an oath of protection for the monks of Mount Sinai. They have the document to this day."

Ari smiled as he looked directly at his brother. "Reza-junam, my dear one, you know my upbringing on a kibbutz wiped away the collected memory of centuries. I am, as always, indebted to you for my re-education."

Reza gently cleared his throat before continuing. "This is, of course, a mosque built by the Fatimids, a Shi'ite dynasty. We, the Mahdi Brotherhood, are always welcome here. However, as you can plainly see, it is not correctly oriented towards Mecca, and is therefore never used as a mosque." He focused his gaze to the left and then the right. "It is at our disposal for as long as we need to be here."

Ari looked at his brother without smiling. "I understand all visitors must leave the compound by twelve noon."

"Yes," Reza replied. "But you and I are not tourists. We can stay here undisturbed for as long as you desire. I have also arranged for our meals to be served here."

"I see," Ari said, even though he did not see, though as the Mahdi, he was supposedly all-knowing and all-powerful. But he knew he had not acquired those occult attributes. His greatest strength lay in his patience and ability to improvise. His weakness lay in his love for Lily and their daughter. *What would Lily say if she could see me now*?

Chapter 8

Thoughts about Ari filled all of Lily's waking hours and even her dreams. This morning she woke heavy-hearted after dreaming of Ari being followed by adoring throngs of men in white robes and turbans. Now fully awake, the memory of how eagerly he had embraced the adulation of the crowd caused her to wince. *Where is he? Why doesn't he return? I could reason with him sitting before me, face to face.*

Abigail, nestled in the bed with her, began mewling softly like a kitten that knows milk is nearby. Lily gently lifted her to her full breasts and let her daughter drink her fill. Fortunately, for all her worry and distress, her milk supply remained abundant.

"What are we going to do today, my darling?" Lily nuzzled the top of her baby's head. "No more sightseeing with Professor Scott, that's for sure." She grunted with revulsion, wanting nothing more to do with the black wraith she had seen near Absalom's tomb.

After the feeding, she washed up and put on a fresh t-shirt and a long denim skirt. She removed Abigail's diaper and gave her a little sponge bath in the bathroom sink.

"Let's go somewhere different for breakfast, okay, sweetheart?" Abigail smiled her big toothless grin in response.

Standing in the square inside Jaffa Gate, Lily weighed her choices. She did not want to eat at the nearby café where she had only recently run into Professor Scott and then Agent Pincus. Neither did she want to go in the direction of the Temple Mount in the Muslim Quarter. She stashed Abigail in the baby sling on her chest, then strode out the gate, turned left and followed the sidewalk along the outer perimeter of the wall. Across the deep valley, she could see the windmill in the neighborhood of Yemin Moshe, and to her right stood the majestic King David Hotel.

"That's where we'll eat breakfast," Lily said with an optimistic lilt in her voice. "We're going to have a full breakfast buffet at the King David, even if it breaks my budget."

Fifteen minutes later, slightly winded from the uphill climb, Lily entered the luxuriously furnished lobby, asked the concierge for directions to the breakfast buffet. By seven a.m., she sat at a table set for one near the window. In the distance, she could discern the outline of the Tower of David at Jaffa Gate. The waiter filled her coffee cup with the strong black liquid which tasted as good as it smelled.

"How old is she?" The waiter beamed in Abigail's direction.

"Six months this week." Lily patted her baby's plump cheek, pleased the waiter had noticed her unusually quiet child.

She then got up and filled her plate at the buffet with bagels, lox, cream cheese, fruit salad, and a hardboiled egg. Later, she had a cup of strawberry yogurt, and fed her daughter a bit of mashed banana.

As Lily sat in the luxurious hotel, she felt the shadow of the previous day evaporate. She knew this was only a temporary reprieve. Nothing had changed, but the affluent atmosphere, along with the infusion of good food provided the uplift her spirits needed—until she caught a glimpse of the young agent who had accompanied Pincus the day before. With mounting chagrin, she watched as he took a table near the window, sitting where he could observe her. The waiter then came and poured him a cup of coffee.

Lily waited for him to go to the buffet table to pick up his breakfast, but the agent evidently did not want to eat. Her thoughts raced. *How can I give him the slip if he just sits there and stares at me?* Then he lifted his cup in her direction and nodded gravely.

What chutzpah! She indignantly turned her head and looked away. Before she could gather her things and slip Abigail into her carrier, she felt, rather than saw, a shadow falling on the remains of her breakfast meal. Sighing deeply, she reluctantly looked up.

"Lily, may I join you?" The agent sat without waiting for her permission. "I just happened to be here this morning when I looked up and saw you there with your lovely daughter." He leaned over and tickled Abigail under the chin.

Lily glared at him. "Cut the pretense. I know Pincus ordered you to spy on me."

"Why would we do that, Lily? You and Ari are not hiding anything from us, now are you?" He smiled benignly then took out a pack of cigarettes and lit one.

"Don't smoke." She nodded her head indicating Abigail.

The agent ground out his cigarette in a saucer. "Forgive me, I wasn't thinking. But to get back to the point of this little visit, we need to know what you and Professor Scott were doing recently in the Kidron Valley."

"You followed us?"

"Of course."

Lily sat momentarily unnerved as she recalled the events of the day before. With effort, she managed to suppress any facial expressions generated by thinking about the wraith at Absalom's Tomb.

"Scott gave me a guided tour of the City of David to distract me from the pressure he felt I was under, what with Ari's absence and your unexpected appearance."

"But you actually never entered the City of David, did you? After getting close to Absalom's Tomb, you suddenly turned back. Why?" The young agent looked straight into her eyes, as if trying to read her thoughts.

Lily laughed nervously and twisted a strand of hair. *Instead of misleading him, or outright lying, why not tell him the truth. He won't believe me, in any case.*

"I saw the shadow of Lucifer." There, she'd said it out loud and the lights did not dim, nor did the table shake.

Caught off-guard by her reply, the man choked back a laugh. He pulled a handkerchief out of his jacket pocket and wiped his mouth. "Lucifer? You are sure of his identity?" A smile appeared on his lips but did not reach his eyes.

"An educated guess," Lily responded, pleased with his apparent amusement at her answer. Let him think her a mental case. It wouldn't be the first time, and if it put him off balance, then good.

Abruptly, the young man stood, mumbled goodbye, and then hurriedly walked out of the dining room while punching a number on his cell phone.

Let him call Pincus. They can now add Lucifer's name to my file. Pincus will probably think it's a code name for someone. I know he never believed my story of the archangel Michael telling me how to save Israel's water supply. Lily's thoughts bounced back and forth from the past to the present as she sat at her table by the window holding Abigail in her lap. The waiter came by, smiled at the baby, and then asked if she needed anything else.

As if waking from a dream, she looked up and shook her head. "We're fine. I just need a few moments to collect myself."

The waiter hesitated then spoke in a soft whisper. "It is not any of my business, but I recognized your visitor as a security agent." He laughed knowingly. "They all dress the same. Are you and your daughter in trouble?"

Lily couldn't repress a smile. Only in Israel would the serving staff even notice her baby daughter, let alone show concern for her safety. Everyone in this country felt free to intervene in her business. Next, she expected the waiter would ask if her daughter could breathe properly in the baby sling. "Thanks for asking, but everything is *beseder*, in order."

The waiter nodded solemnly then turned back to his duties at other tables. Lily left a large tip, more than she could afford, and exited the King David. Not knowing where to go and what to do, she crossed the street and walked past the YMCA, built she noted, with the same kind of Jerusalem golden limestone as the King David. Sensing she might be under surveillance, she abruptly turned into the gardens of the YMCA compound. Hearing violins, she followed the sound until she came to a large concert hall.

Curious as to who held a concert so early in the morning, she stepped inside the hall and slipped into a seat in the back row. Musicians stood on the stage, evidently rehearsing for a performance. A man and woman sang a duet as two violins and a cello accompanied them. The song sounded hauntingly sad, and at the same time pleasing to the ear. Lily realized they were singing in Hebrew, but did not recognize the song.

Abigail fell asleep in her arms and snored softly. As if mesmerized by the music, Lily too nodded off in a light doze. In this peaceful state, the archangel Michael appeared to her once again. "Do not be afraid, Lily. Go to the place called the House of Prayer."

Lily didn't know how long she slept, but when she opened her eyes, the stage appeared empty and the musicians were gone. She remained in the now-darkened auditorium. A deep sense of abiding peace suffused her entire being. *All is well. I will find this house of prayer, then return to Tiberias and wait for Ari.*

Chapter 9

Ari turned back and gazed one last time on the monastery nestled in the cliffs of Mount Sinai. His time of seclusion with his brother Reza had come to an end, and now the two of them were heading for the Red Sea resort of Sharm al Sheik. While seated in the back seat of a Land Rover, he patted the inner pocket in his black tunic that held his new identity papers. He would re-enter Israel through the Taba border crossing using the name of Brother Lucas of the Greek Orthodox faith. He had in his possession a genuine invitation from the Patriarch of Jerusalem offering him a place of humble service in the small property the church owned in Silwan. Reza had explained the church owned an orchard that included a small house for the caretaker. Muslims inhabited most of the village, situated in a *wadi* south of the Temple Mount, along with a sprinkling of Jews associated with the newly excavated City of David. In these simple surroundings, the Mahdi would begin his return to Jerusalem.

The two brothers rode in silence as the driver expertly and with great speed drove south to Sharm al Sheik. The silence and enigma of the harsh Sinai desert gradually vanished as the opulent resort town appeared in the distance with the blue waters of the Red Sea breaking the monotone of the landscape. Here the brothers took leave of each other, with Reza returning to Cairo, and then on to France.

Dressed in the black tunic of a Greek Orthodox monk, Ari passed through customs and security without incident. His passport, stamped with an authentic entry visa for visiting clergy, raised no eyebrows on either side of the border. He hired a taxi to take him to the central bus station in Eilat. Both he and Reza agreed having a driver and vehicle waiting for him at the border crossing would only cause suspicion. Ari, now posing as a low-ranking monk traveling to his next assignment, would live in great simplicity as the caretaker of an overgrown garden.

Waiting for the bus to Jerusalem, Ari indulged his Israeli appetite with a falafel, the pita stuffed with chopped vegetables, topped with fried potatoes and tahina sauce. Wiping a bit of sauce off his chin, he automatically scanned the waiting room, looking for the anomalies that warned of danger. No one paid attention to him, dressed as a Christian monk, his long curly hair tied back in a ponytail. Most of his fellow travelers were young people wearing t-shirts and shorts. A middle-aged American couple, both attired in linen pants and Hawaiian shirts, sat beside him. Finished with his snack, Ari looked straight ahead, not wishing to engage the couple in conversation, even as they stared pointedly in his direction.

The six-hour journey took him past the remains of Sodom and Gomorra, the luxury resort hotels on the Dead Sea, and the green oasis of Ein Gedi. One of the few pleasant memories Ari had of his time as a soldier in the Israeli Army had been an off-duty hike in the *wadi* above Ein Gedi. There, he swam in deep pools of cold water. He recalled how the curious conies peered out from the rocks, and gazelles scrambled from cleft to cleft with sure, nimble hoofs. David, before he even dreamt of being a king, used to roam through this *wadi* with his companions. They most likely swam in the very same pool beneath the waterfall.

Ari shrugged ruefully, as he remembered his earlier life which seemed to have been so uncomplicated. Back then, as a raw, young soldier undergoing basic training, he never envisioned the role he would one day play as the Muslim messiah. *Did young David, as he hid from the army of King Saul, know one day he would rule a large kingdom?*

The bus rushed by the oasis of Ein Gedi, and then began climbing upward as the road continued on to Jerusalem. Ari knew instinctively not to enter Jerusalem triumphantly, as the Holy One—the long-awaited Hidden Mahdi. No, he would enter the city as a lowly monk of the Greek Orthodox branch of Christianity. At least he had the satisfaction of knowing this would be the final chapter, here in the village of Silwan, otherwise known as the ancient City of David. He would eventually leave the Greek Orthodox garden, at the set time, at the moment preordained. Until then, he would play out this role with patience.

The only shadow on his mind was the place his beloved wife and baby daughter played in this scenario. He could not reconcile the two roles, husband and father, with the messiah who would bring peace to the world through the rule of Islam. While on Mount Sinai, he had finally accepted he was in fact the Mahdi. No longer did he consider the idea absurd or simply a case of mistaken identity.

As the bus passed through the tunnel between the Mount of Olives and Mount Scopus, Ari sat up straighter, shook his head, and flexed his hands to refocus his mind. He needed all his wits about him as he returned to Jerusalem. The bus pulled into the central station and all passengers disembarked. He walked through the terminal, and out to Jaffa Road where he took the only bus to the Dung Gate. Most of his fellow passengers were Orthodox Jews on their way to pray at the Western Wall.

At the final destination, the men wearing *tefillin* stepped off and walked through the Dung Gate. Ari, dressed in a cassock, turned and followed a narrow lane into the village of Silwan. On his left, he observed the entrance to the archaeological park open to the public, now called the City of David. He continued down the lane, remembering his instructions from Reza. Halfway down, he recognized the bakery which sold flat bread and round, crusty *begaleh*. The familiar aroma of roasted sesame seeds filled his nostrils. From there he entered a narrow alley that wound between stone houses built one on top of the other. Little boys, shouted in high-pitched Arabic, kicked a soccer ball between their feet, and paid no attention to the monk.

Ari proceeded, as were his instructions, to the end of the alley. Now, standing in front of a wooden gate set in a mud-brick wall, he pulled on the bell rope, and waited in the blazing sun. He glanced at his watch as the minutes passed. He rang the bell again, and then bowed his head in resignation, maintaining his disguise as a humble monk stationed at a derelict and disregarded mission station.

After a long five minutes, the gate creaked slowly open and the old man standing before him looked up at him with rheumy eyes. Ari sized up his host and his immediate surroundings and pursed his lips, acknowledging his brother Reza knew how to hide a personage like the Mahdi. Nobody would look for him here, not his enemies in Qom or Mecca, nor the spies from the Vatican, not even the Mossad. In the heart of the City of David, just outside the walls of the Old City, he would set in motion the events to bring the world to him.

"*Ahlan wasahlan*, welcome," the gatekeeper said. Ari noted he did not bow his head, as he would have if he had known who stood before him.

Looking over his shoulder to make sure he had not been followed, Ari stepped inside the compound. The old man led him to a shady grape arbor and motioned for him to sit on a chair made of wicker. Then he went inside the small house, presumably to make the requisite glass of tea.

Ari put down his satchel and looked around him with curiosity. To his left he could make out the ruins of the City of David. To the north of the garden he noticed a small mosque with its minaret towering over all. Below him, the ground sloped down to a much-neglected orchard. He looked forward to investigating what kind of fruit trees grew there. He laughed quietly, acknowledging that his kibbutz upbringing had not been wasted.

"You find the view pleasing?" the old man appeared by his side with a tray and one glass of tea.

"Yes, my dear man. I love fruit." He took the proffered glass. "What should I call you?" Ari could tell by the man's worn blue jeans, faded black shirt, and shorn hair that he was not a fellow monk.

"I am called George." He nodded gravely and added. "My father, may he rest in peace, also called George, as is my son and first grandson."

"Do they live nearby?" Ari asked out of politeness rather than interest.

"Down the *wadi* past Ein Rogel. I will retire there also, now that you have come to guard and maintain the garden."

"There seems to have been very little maintenance done in the last few years." As soon as the words were out of his mouth, Ari realized he had insulted old George, which had not been his intention. To mollify him he added, "Of course, it is too much work for one man." To change the subject, he inquired about the neighbors on the right and left of the enclosed garden.

George's expression never changed, but he lifted his eyes and looked to the left. "The Jews, rebuilding what they call the City of David, treat us with respect. In fact, the man in charge has already spoken with the Archbishop about digging a trench across the orchard below us. He thinks the ancient pool of Siloam is partially under our land."

Ari's eyes narrowed with apprehension. It would not be good for him to have Israelis messing around in this property. They would surely recognize his Hebrew accented Arabic. "Has permission been granted?"

Old George snorted in reply. "What do you think? The Archbishop will keep him waiting for years with neither a yes or no."

"Why is that?" Ari's amused look implied he already knew the answer, but in fact it was an honest question.

"We have to placate the Palestinians. This village is ninety percent Muslim. We have always gotten along with the mullah next door." He turned and looked at the mosque.

Ari placed his empty glass on the tray. "Show me around, and you can get back to your family all the sooner."

The little house beside the grape arbor consisted of one room containing a bed and one chair with an old-fashioned wardrobe and a small sink. The cooking facilities, outside but sheltered by a roof, consisted of a two-ring gas cooker attached to a tank. The outhouse stood in a far corner. Not much different from the monastery where Lily and he had hidden for over a year.

Ari placed his bag on the foot of the bed and walked George to the garden gate. "After I get settled in and learn my duties here, I will visit your home beyond Ein Rogel."

The old man gravely shook his hand before replying, "You are always welcome." He turned and walked out the gate and up the alley Ari had so recently passed. Abruptly, he paused, as if he'd just thought of something. Turning back to look at Ari still standing at the open gate, he called back, "Peace be with you, brother."

"And with you," Ari called back. As he shut the gate and securely bolted the bar in place, a sense of disquiet and unease descended over him. Why did the old man seem so anxious to leave? This bit of neglected property, forgotten and almost abandoned by the church, did not appear to have much significance. That is precisely why Reza had arranged for Ari to live here. No one would think it suspicious for a Greek Orthodox monk to tend the orchard and grapevines.

Suddenly weary from his long journey from the Sinai, through the Negev, and now in East Jerusalem, Ari took off his rumpled black cassock and lay down on the bed. He briefly noticed with gratitude the pillowcase appeared freshly laundered, starched and ironed, no doubt by George's wife or granddaughter. As soon as his head hit the pillow, he fell into a deep sleep.

The shadows crept across the city and even the call to evening prayer issuing from the nearby mosque did not wake Ari. Near dawn, with the birds awake and twittering among the branches, he heard the morning call to prayer. He sat up startled, temporarily not knowing where he was. He looked around the room expecting to see Lily. Disappointed, he rubbed his eyes, remembering there was no way Lily and Abigail could join him here. Not only was he masquerading as a celibate monk, but from here, the Mahdi would take control of the Temple Mount. His wife and child were safe in their cottage in Tiberias, and there they would remain until his reign solidified. He had not, and would not abandon them, even though he knew Lily might think that now.

Rolling out of the bed, he realized here in the Greek Orthodox garden he would not be waited on by faithful servants as he had on the backside of the Mount of Olives. No special treats would be flown in just for his enjoyment. He splashed cold water on his face from the small basin. After dressing, he went out to the lean-to which served as a kitchen and brewed a pot of Turkish coffee. It would do until he learned where the nearest bakery and grocery shops were located. He knew every village and neighborhood in the Middle East had its small shops that supplied the day-to-day needs of people who could not afford to do weekly shopping in large supermarkets.

First, he would survey his new domain by walking the perimeter of the property to inspect the walls and get a sense of his new neighbors. He started at the top of the walled garden, where he found a locked gate. Looking over the wall he could see the white domed roof of the nearby mosque. This could be a convenient location for his followers to gain access to him without being seen. He wondered if old George had left a key in the cottage, and who else owned a key to this gate.

The terraced garden took advantage of the steep slope of the hillside. Here, untended grape vines withered on the stakes, unlike the lush grape arbor which gave shelter from the sun on the patio beside the house. In former days, when more than one caretaker had lived here, this garden must have supplied grapes and other fruits to the Archbishop's household.

Moving on to lower levels, his view of his immediate neighbors was blocked by the mud brick wall. But he knew Israeli archaeologists were burrowing deep into the hillside, uncovering layer after layer of the ancient neighborhood long ago inhabited by King David. Already a major tourist destination, hundreds of curious pilgrims entered the large complex of underground caves and tunnels. Many years earlier, Ari had waded through the knee-deep water in Hezekiah's tunnel. They must have found much since then.

He continued downward, assessing the strength of the wall, looking for any breaches which could be used by those out to destroy him. He began to think like his brother Reza, who knew not all Muslims welcomed the arrival of the Mahdi. Political realities of absolute power and vast wealth convinced most leaders they did not want to change the status quo. No, the Mahdi had to be discreet and devious until his time came to appear in power and glory.

At the lower quarter of the property, the land leveled out and he found an almond grove, much neglected and in need of drastic pruning, but nonetheless a fine old grove. Ari's instinct, as a farmer and son of the kibbutz, was to inspect the trees first. But his sense of urgency compelled him to inspect this portion of the wall. In fact, the brick wall ended here and only a barbed wire fence separated him from the property next door. Hiding in the shadow of a fig tree, he peered across the fence. He could see a spring of water overflowed down broad stone steps that led to an ancient pool. This must be the pool of Siloam George had spoken of. The Israelis needed permission from the Archbishop to dig on this side of the barbed wire fence. Ari hoped it would never happen during his time here.

Ari put out his hand and plucked a ripe fig, purple and bursting with juice. No sooner had he wiped the juice off his lips he saw a familiar figure standing on the steps opposite. Stepping backwards into the foliage, he peered intently across the divide at the face of Professor Scott. When had he seen him last? At Banias, of course, that fateful day when Lily had thrown the petrified almond twig into the churning water thereby negating the toxins placed there by terrorists. What brought Scott here now? How did he always manage to show up at such pivotal moments in their lives? *Is this a good omen? Is this a curse?*

While Ari stood still as a statue beneath the fig tree on the border between the two properties, an older man with a thick mane of snow-white hair approached Scott and engaged him in conversation. Ari could not make out what they were talking about but surmised it had to do with the ongoing excavations.

Ari waited for the two men to leave the area. It would be most unfortunate if Scott looked across the fence and recognized him. Sadly, Ari accepted he would have to forgo the pleasure of pruning the almond trees in this portion of the garden. They could not and must not encounter each other.

When he felt safe, he continued his walk around the perimeter of the property, gradually ending at the upper level. He made another cup of coffee and drank it while sitting under the grape arbor. It was a waiting game, always waiting. He felt like a chess piece being strategically moved forward or backward. But whose hand did the moving? Ari bolstered his courage with this and similar thoughts as the morning sun moved across the pale blue sky. This unexpected appearance of Professor Scott had thrown him off course mentally. After having spent so much time with Muslims on the Mount of Olives and Mount Sinai, he now felt conflicted with all Scott represented. Western scientific thought and philosophy did not sit well with the ideology of the Mahdi Brotherhood. In fact, it stood as its antithesis.

Furthermore, Lily trusted Scott and considered him a friend. He had never done anything to betray their secrets or harm them in any way. In fact, he had been very instrumental in helping Lily find the burial cave in Ain Karem. Without his help she would not have discovered the almond twig or the two sacramental stones. Ari knew she still carried them with her in a small pouch around her neck. The stones guided her in situations of perplexity and doubt, revealing which way to go.

Loneliness swept over him as he thought of his wife. *What would I give to have her beside me now?* Gathering every ounce of will power, Ari forced himself to remember his mission and the danger it entailed for Lily and Abigail. When the time came for him to reveal himself to the world, then and only then could they safely join him.

Chapter 10

The tall, gaunt gardener went about his daily task at the Scottish Guest House in Tiberias as if he were an invisible man. The brim of his straw hat hid his rugged features as effectively as any mask. His faded and much-mended work shirt and trousers blended into oblivion beneath the overhanging foliage. His gnarly, soil encrusted feet, encased in dilapidated sandals disappeared in the dust. Patrons of the Guest House overlooked him entirely and fellow employees, the maids, cooks and waiters deliberately ignored him.

And that is how Yusef wanted it. Years ago, when still young enough to have had some modicum of ambition in life, the Mahdi Brotherhood recruited him to their cause. Growing up in Nazareth, where the Christian Arabs dominated the lower city and the Jews the upper, a root of bitterness grew out of the bleakness of his worldly prospects. Until the day when a man came all the way from Persia and filled his mind and heart with longing for a purer, higher calling.

His first assignment, which turned out to be his only assignment, appeared to be somewhat of a disappointment for a young man who wanted to accomplish something big. Through this Persian's mysterious contacts in the Roman Catholic Church, Yusef became the caretaker of Saint Peter's church on the shore of the Sea of Galilee. It turned out to be an old, historic church, with one Franciscan priest and no congregation to speak of, since the Christian Arabs had left Tiberias long before.

Father Philip tried to renovate the church and its adjacent hostel, but funds were lacking and his superiors in Jerusalem had no ambitions for the site, other than to hold on to it for eternity. Jewish-owned restaurants sprang up on the boardwalk in front and on either side of the church, effectively hiding it from public view. As the years passed, residents and tourists alike forgot a church on the waterfront existed.

Father Philip welcomed the young man from Nazareth and kept him employed from morning till night painting, plastering, sweeping, and tending the plants in the inner courtyard. He paid him a small stipend plus room and board. But as the years passed, and the Mahdi Brotherhood never gave him a task or mission to perform, his hopes faded.

Then, when he heard of a better-paying position as chief gardener at the Scottish Guest House, he did not hesitate to change his position and turn his loyalties from the Roman Catholic Church to the Protestant Church. Father Philip, briefly puzzled by his choice, said nothing. Yusef had always kept to himself, as if harboring a deep secret. The kindly priest had hoped one day to be let into his confidence, but that was not to be.

The people in charge at the Scotty, as the local population called it, did not give Yusef a second thought. He did his job, lived quietly in one small room located in the back garden and slowly slipped in to a life of anonymity, until today.

Yusef's heart pounded in his chest and perspiration beaded his lined forehead when he heard a knock on his door. No one had ever come to his room before, not once in all the years he'd toiled in the gardens. He wiped his sweaty palms on his trousers and peered out the small, dirty window in the door. The night was dark, but a waxing moon cast enough light so he could make out the prominent features of a fellow Arab.

"Fatimah sends her respects." The slender man with a large mustache spoke barely above a whisper.

The blood drained from Yusef's face as he heard the secret password spoken. Why now? What use could he possibly be in his old age, and finally content with his lot? At the same time, something in him welled up with gratitude and pride that the Mahdi Brotherhood had not forgotten him. They took the trouble to find him in the secluded back gardens of the Scottish Guest House. Panic gripped his throat as he struggled to remember the reply he had been instructed to give after just such a greeting. How did it go? Something about Ali, yes, that was it.

"Ali responds in kind." Yusef spoke in a quivering voice which betrayed his emotion.

"Are you going to keep me standing out here all night?"

The door opened, and Yusef bid the man enter. After he heard what his visitor had to say, his life changed irrevocably. Yusef, not a trained assassin, and incapable of slitting anyone's throat, especially those of a woman and small child, was obviously unsuited for the task. His visitor recognized this flaw immediately, and with hardly a pause outlined a contingency plan.

"You will arrange for the propane tanks that supply the kitchen to explode, demolishing the entire house, killing everyone inside. Is that clear? Can you manage to do such a simple task? Or do I need to find another servant to do the will of the Holy One?"

Yusef held his breath. He was not so simple that he did not hear the implied threat to his own life. He would undertake this mission or be eliminated from the ranks of the Brotherhood. Forcing himself to control the trembling of his limbs, he cleared his throat and replied. "Just say when."

"Good. Thanks be to Allah. The intended target is now in Jerusalem. When she arrives home, you will give her time to settle in. Take this bag. It contains the address, photographs of the target and explosive material to aid in the detonation."

Yusef never saw his visitor again. That very night he began surveillance of the small cottage situated only two lanes away from the Scotty. Days passed before he saw a light in the window of the cottage. Then he prepared his explosives and carried out his first and only mission. At six a.m., the blast rocked the neighborhood. Yusef gathered with the curious onlookers and disheveled neighbors who rushed out to see the damage. He nodded with satisfaction when he heard a woman say the occupants of the house were burned beyond recognition.

Chapter 11

Life fell into a regular routine for Ari as he continued to live the life of a humble monk, posing as the caretaker of a Greek Orthodox garden in a backwater of Jerusalem. No one in his immediate neighborhood had any inkling about his true identity. He went shopping and bought his own bread, cheese, tomatoes, and cucumbers like everyone else. No visitors appeared at his gate at the end of the lane. The boys who kicked their soccer ball back and forth between the houses never bothered to even look up when he passed by.

Late one night, when most residents of Silwan had turned out their lights and gone to sleep, bearded men dressed in black silently gathered at the mosque which sat opposite the upper wall of the Greek property. They did not come to pray. They came to pay homage to the Mahdi and listen to his wisdom, preparing themselves for the day when he would show himself to the religious leaders at the Al Aksa Mosque, then to the Jews and Christians living in Jerusalem, and then to the ends of the earth.

They startled Ari the first time they appeared. After midnight, he heard soft footsteps in the garden. Slipping the knife from under his pillow, he crept to the window, peering into the darkness. His night vision abilities were above average, which enabled him to see shadows and shapes in the dark which most could not see. Three men approached his cottage. Their hands were empty, and it did not appear they had concealed weapons, although they could have had knives hidden under their tunics. Their pace held steady, without stealth or subtlety.

"Fatimah greets you, your Excellency," one of the three spoke aloud.

Ari recognized the code words and stepped back from the window, at the same time reaching for his black robe lying across the foot of his bed. Slipping it over his head, he went to the door. His fingers trembled as he turned the key in the lock. "Ali responds in kind," he replied through the crack in the door. *Why had they not warned him they would be coming this night?*

He turned on the electric light bulb which hung from the ceiling. Feeling outnumbered and exposed, he took a deep breath and beckoned his visitors to enter.

They stood awkwardly in a semicircle, not that they would have sat in the presence of the Mahdi without his permission even if there had been enough chairs.

Ari quickly took command of the situation, and not because he instinctively knew what to do, nor would he venture to guess why they had come out of nowhere in the darkness. Rather, his gut instinct told him to present himself as their undisputed leader. He still had much to learn about this business of being the Mahdi. His brother Reza had instructed him as much as possible during their time in the Sinai, but even Reza had always assumed Ari would know when and how to act for each occasion.

"So, you came from the mosque?" Ari hazarded a guess, keeping all expression out of his face.

"Yes, your Excellency," a man with a long, white beard replied.

"You have a key to the gate." Ari said, making a statement, not a question.

"We have." The three men nodded together.

And why do I not have a key? Of course, the Mahdi can appear anywhere, not using gates or doors. I have not yet learned how to manifest this occult power, but I must not let on.

"Why have you come?" Ari said, intentionally abrupt.

The men looked momentarily puzzled. "You summoned us."

Thinking quickly, Ari replied, "You mean Reza ordered you to pay this visit."

"Yes," the older man spoke haltingly. "Have we displeased you?"

Ari saw fear in the old man's eyes, and quickly reassured him.

"I wanted to see how fast you could respond. I have nothing to say to you tonight. Go in peace." Ari saw a visible wave of relief sweep through his visitors.

The three men slipped out into the garden and returned to the mosque via the upper gate. Ari sat up for the rest of the night in a state of agitation. This messiah business was not going to be as easy a calling as he had envisioned while sitting in the rarified air of Mount Sinai. Here in Jerusalem, among the rank and file of ordinary human beings, the way was not so clear. *Did Jesus of Nazareth have such doubts? In any case, it ended badly for the Nazarene.* Finally, Ari lay down to sleep. With his mind troubled, he sought the oblivion sleep would bring, if only temporarily.

Just before noon, the sound of the bell ringing at his front gate woke him. After a quick splash of cold water on his face, he slipped on his black cassock, shoved his feet into sandals, and hurried to the gate, where the bell tolled incessantly.

"All right," he shouted. "Quit ringing the bell." He opened the small window in the gate to ascertain who was demanding his attention. Peering through the small opening, he saw no one.

"Who is there?" He spoke in English rather than Hebrew or Arabic. His knowledge of Greek was zero, but

Reza had assured him it was not uncommon to have American-born monks in the Greek Orthodox community.

Two giggling girls stepped back from the wall where he could see them through the opening. Both were carrying baskets covered with linen cloths. They held them up in the universal gesture of a gift being offered.

"Our father sends this for your lunch," the taller of the two girls said in Arabic. Her dark brown hair, plaited on both sides of her narrow face, and her large, black eyes shone with excitement.

"George?"

"*Aywa*, yeah," she replied, and then proceeded to giggle again.

Ari released the bolt on the inside. No unexpected visitors would enter the garden from this entrance, he noted with approval. The two girls, about eight and ten years of age, and wearing cotton dresses over trousers, eyed each other. They handed him the two baskets, then skipped out the open gate like two young gazelles.

Ari lifted a linen cover and smiled as the aroma of freshly baked sesame rolls, sprinkled with *za'atar,* reached his nostrils. In addition to the bread, he saw three hard-boiled eggs. When he returned to the cottage, he lit the gas ring to make Turkish coffee. The second basket held tomatoes and small, crisp cucumbers, the ubiquitous staple of the Middle Eastern diet.

Eating his first meal of the day on the patio under the grape arbor, Ari's perspective of his mission improved tenfold from how he'd felt the night before when he'd received his visitors. "This stage of the enterprise is going to be more pleasant than I thought." He had no inkling what the end of the day would bring.

* * * *

Ari put all his energy into pruning the neglected fruit trees in the lower garden, being careful to stay on the side opposite the excavations next door. He did not want to risk being seen by Scott or anyone else. The work was hard but satisfying. Everything he had learned on his kibbutz came in handy. He realized with some satisfaction he would have made a good agriculturist if fate had not intervened and set him on another course.

At the end of the day, tired and dirty, he washed under the shower tap behind the cottage, grateful a previous monk had taken the trouble to install a solar panel which supplied all the hot water he needed and then some. He ate the remains of the food George's daughters had dropped off earlier that day. The small meal reminded him he needed to do some shopping tomorrow. He would need to buy bread, cheese, salami, and fresh fruit and vegetables. All this he knew he could obtain at a nearby grocery shop in the village where his presence would not be questioned.

Just before retiring for the night, he took one last walk around the upper garden, breathing in the fragrance of the night blooming jasmine which grew over the wall. Passing the upper gate, behind which stood the mosque, he reached out a hand to reassure himself it was securely locked. *I must change this arrangement. I cannot have these men dropping in unexpected and uninvited.* The moon cast just enough light so he could see the gate clearly. A hint of something white on the ground below caught his attention. Cautiously, he stepped back thinking it could be an explosive device. No, it seemed to be a white envelope. That too could be dangerous, since letter bombs were a favorite tool of certain groups. Stepping closer, he gingerly ran a forefinger lightly over the envelope. Feeling nothing metallic which could trigger an explosion, he lifted it by one corner.

Returning to the cottage, he set the missive on the table. It was not the first time he'd received an unwanted communication. He remembered the letter which had reached him in the desert of the American Southwest. That letter had sent him and Lily running for their lives.

He squared his shoulders, took a deep breath, and determined to stay his ground, no matter what news the letter might bring. He took a kitchen knife, slit the envelope, and shook out the contents. A single newspaper clipping drifted down and rested on the table.

He picked it up and began reading. As his eyes scanned the Hebrew newsprint, the blood drained from his face leaving him light-headed, and then he slumped down on a chair. Not believing what he had just read, he picked it up and read again the brief account of a propane explosion that destroyed a house in Tiberias. The current occupants, a woman and child, had burned to death, and the husband was missing.

Chapter 12

Ari could shed no more tears. A blank numbness encased his heart and mind. Days passed when he never got out of bed. The restoration of the orchard forgotten, the fruit trees left once again to languish. He neither trimmed his beard nor combed his hair. The thought of food revolted him, but even if he had been hungry, he had purchased no food supplies. No visitors came to the main gate or the secondary gate in the upper garden. His robe smelled rank, as did his unwashed body.

On the third day of mourning for his wife and child, Ari crawled out of his soiled, tangled sheets, gulped down a glass of water, and stumbled out to the terrace. Sharp hunger pangs drove him to find nourishment, overriding his shut-down emotional state. But even hunger could not stifle the sense of self-preservation which prevented him from stumbling out into the village in his current condition. With unsure steps, he followed the footpath down toward the fig tree that grew on the border of the Greek property and the pool of Siloam. He vaguely remembered having eaten a juicy fig that first day when he had spotted Professor Scott through the barbed wire fence.

The birds had eaten most of the ripe figs, especially on the upper branches, but pushing back the lower branches and reaching deep within the foliage, he plucked a handful of the sweet fruit, stuffing it into his mouth like a starving man. Momentarily sated, his eyes brightened even as the sticky pulp covered his lips. Wiping his hands on his robe, he peered through the leaves to see if anyone had observed him. Spotting no one at the site, he retreated up the hillside to the cottage.

With his mind clearer than it had been for the previous three days, he put on the kettle to make a cup of strong coffee. While waiting for the water to boil, he contemplated his options. He had no reason to return to Tiberias. Lily and Abigail's remains would have been buried, by Jewish custom, within twenty-four hours of death. The police, and God only knew who else, would be looking for him. The newspaper clipping had implied a faulty gas tube might have been responsible for the explosion, and the double tragedy might have been an accident.

But was it an accident? Ari knew the Mahdi Brotherhood had no use for Lily, and they did not understand his love for her. But hadn't the Prophet Mohammed benefited financially from the marriage to his first wife Khadija? And hadn't he deeply loved his fourth wife, Aisha? There is precedent in the Mahdi having need of a spouse, if only temporarily. Ari knew his brother Reza feared Lily's power, somehow intuiting her connection to the archangel Michael. *But would he have ordered her death?*

Maybe Pincus was involved. Ari could not believe the Mossad agent would deliberately harm Lily and his daughter but maybe, some order had gone amiss and instead of protecting them, they had been killed. But the more Ari thought about it, the more he came to believe his original theory. There was a traitor inside the Mossad. Lily had somehow stumbled onto his identity. That would explain why she had to be taken out. Abigail, of course, had just been collateral damage. Ari choked back a sob as he said his daughter's name, "Abby, my little dove."

Ari chose to privately honor their deaths by observing the full seven days of mourning. He neither bathed nor shaved during this period, eating only the fruit from the garden, and drinking tap water or hot, bitter coffee. His cheeks became gaunt, but his eyes burned with an inner light fueled by the desire for revenge.

At the end of the seven days, he bathed, trimmed his beard, combed his hair and tied it back in a monk's bun. After putting on a freshly laundered robe he stepped outside the gate to once again engage with the world around him. The boys, who normally hung around the lane kicking a ball, were evidently now in school. He passed no one on his way to the neighborhood grocery. A grizzled old Palestinian, sitting on a stool behind the counter, did not even look up when Ari came in to his store. He purchased onions, tomatoes, cucumbers, yellow cheese, bread, and a bottle of wine. He considered a bag of rice then shrugged and put it down.

"Where can I get a good meal around here?" Ari asked the proprietor.

The old man looked up and appraised his customer, taking in his apparel as well as his demeanor. "Abu Ziad's restaurant." He inclined his head to one side. "Up the street. You will not miss it."

Carrying his purchases in a cloth bag, Ari returned to his cottage and waited impatiently for the midday sun to reach its zenith. Shortly after two p.m., Ari made his way up the street to Abu Ziad's kebob shop. It consisted of a few wooden tables behind a flyspecked window. In a small courtyard out back, the mouth-watering aroma of grilled meat wafted through the air. Ari took a seat at one of the tables, as always choosing a chair that faced the door. The customers were all young males. The married men evidently went home for their meal. The men looked up when he entered the shop, took in his appearance from head to toe, then went back to their private conversations.

Ari forced himself to eat slowly, not only to savor the first real food he'd had in over a week, but so as not to attract attention. A ravenous monk would arouse suspicion, as everyone knew the clergy dined well. He chewed each morsel of tender lamb between the bites of saffron rice. He rolled the thin, flat bread in half and dipped it in a dish of creamy *leban*. When he'd finished his plate, he pushed it back and waited for the glass of mint tea which always followed such a meal.

Ari caught the eye of the owner, who watched him closely. He drank his tea, paid his bill, and left no tip. Walking casually, as a monk would after eating a big meal, he felt inexplicably drawn to the nearby Temple Mount. It had been a long time since he had been there. Adroitly, he maneuvered between the cars and tour buses which clogged the street outside the nearby Dung Gate. Mingling with a crowd of tourists he entered the square before the Western Wall. High above the stones that Suleiman's builders had put in place, he gazed at the golden dome of the mosque.

What would Lily have thought about my decision to accept my destiny? He could not help thinking of her now, even though he had to acknowledge she would have vehemently opposed his choice. And yes, he reminded himself, it was a choice to take on the role of the Mahdi. He could have disappeared permanently. Why had he returned to Israel? Why not South America? They could have lost themselves in the jungles of the Amazon, or the rugged regions of Australia's outback. His brother, Reza, would never have found them there. Now she was dead, along with his daughter, and he stood on the terrace before the Western Wall, watching and waiting.

Ari moved through the crowd of Jewish worshipers and curious tourists as if he were invisible, which he nearly was, dressed in the black robe of a Greek monk. Taking a shortcut down several narrow lanes he approached the gate where Muslims entered the Temple Mount to pray at the mosque. Three Border Patrol officers and one Arab policeman stood or sat on stools near the entrance, admitting Muslims while politely refusing entrance to Christians or Jews. *How do they know who is what?* Ari looked down at his clerical robe. Not only clothing revealed nationality and religion, the soldiers on duty had obviously been trained to ask the right questions and listen for accents as well as familiarity with Muslim religious observance.

Realizing he would never be admitted to the Temple courtyard, he took the first turn just before the entrance, walking head down with arms folded until he reached the Via Dolorosa. He kept moving, one foot before the other, oblivious to the history of the Way of Sorrow upon which he walked. His official period of mourning had ended, but his grief, lodged like a slab of cold marble in his chest, gave no evidence of going away.

Chapter 13

Leaving the Old City through Jaffa Gate, Lily turned right and followed the sidewalk as far as Damascus Gate. She stood facing the Mount of Olives to the east, and debated whether to continue her search for this so-called house of prayer the archangel had directed her to find, or be sensible and return home to Tiberias. Pedestrians swirled about her and Abby as she continued to stand there. She remained so long the street vendors began to give her curious looks beneath their bushy eyebrows. Abruptly making up her mind, she crossed the road, and continued past the Garden Tomb. In front of Saint George's School for Boys, she stopped once again to get her bearings. Feeling overwhelmed by the unrelenting heat, she stopped to wipe the perspiration off her face with the back of a hand when she heard a voice speak her name.

"Lily, what a surprise," Professor Scott said as he stood by an open gate. "What are you doing wandering around in the heat of the day?" He wore cargo shorts, leather sandals and a short-sleeved white shirt, open at the collar in the Israeli manner.

Peering behind him, Lily could see a portion of an old-fashioned mansion situated in the midst of a large garden. She recognized it as a relic of the British Mandate era.

"You live here?" Her eyes widened in awe.

"Don't you remember? I mentioned I have an old house in East Jerusalem. My university is leasing it as a future dig house. You know, for the day when undergraduates will once again be allowed to come to the

Middle East." He sighed, as if in doubt of such an eventuality, then shrugged and smiled at her. "Come in and have a cold drink."

Once inside, the coolness of the high-ceilinged entrance hall felt good. She followed Scott into a large kitchen in the back of the house. He gestured for her to take a seat at the round table which could seat ten people, while he took a pitcher of lemonade from the refrigerator.

"You live here alone?" Lily had never seen such a large refrigerator in any kitchen in all of Israel. She slipped Abigail out of the sling and dangled her on her lap.

"That's right, but only until students are allowed to come over. Before my university bought it from the Baptists it was called The House of Prayer for All Nations," he explained.

"The House of Prayer," Lily mumbled. Stunned by the coincidence, she tried to hide her confusion by taking a long sip from the glass of lemonade.

"Finish your drink, and I'll give you a tour of the place." Scott spoke with the humble yet self-confident tone peculiar to Americans. Now more than curious, Lily decided to go along. Maybe, the other rooms would reveal more about why she was meant to be here.

Scott showed her his office, then a spacious reception room. After that, he led her up the stairs to the second floor.

"The entire left wing is a private apartment. I bunk there at present."

He did not open the door to his quarters but instead he took her into a small hallway, and then asked her to remove her shoes.

"Why?" Lily tilted her head in amusement.

"Behind this door is the prayer room."

"A mosque?" Lily looked surprised.

Scott smiled. "Not only Muslims remove their shoes before entering a holy place."

Embarrassed, Lily complied and placed her sandals in a small cubby provided for the purpose. She followed the professor through a wide doorway into a large room. The floor was carpeted in thick wool, and huge cushions lay piled about in random positions. Then she saw the six-foot wooden cross hanging on the opposite wall.

Lily stood in awkward silence. Raised Jewish, she felt at a loss as to how to react in the presence of a cross, especially one as large as this one. She spied a mound of pillows in the far corner, turned her back on the cross, and told Scott she needed a moment alone to feed her child. He nodded in understanding and left the room. Cradling her daughter in her arms, she reclined on the floor cushions taking advantage of the privacy to open her blouse and allow her child to nurse. Eventually, she stretched her legs to relieve a muscle cramp, as she gradually surveyed the prayer room. *Why has the archangel Michael directed me here?*

When Abigail was full and vigorously burped, Lily stood up, straightened her clothing, and positioned the baby back in the sling.

Leaving the prayer room, she slipped on her sandals, and then proceeded downstairs where she discovered Scott now in his study.

He beamed at the two of them, as if nothing could have pleased him more. "Let's see if I can brew up a pot of coffee to wash down the cinnamon rolls I bought early this morning." He herded them into the sunlit kitchen like a beneficent shepherd.

"When are you returning home?" Scott asked, as he gazed into her eyes with a piercing look.

Lily wanted to tell him everything, but something made her hold back, maybe because Scott was *too* kind. "We were going back today." Her voice trailed off in doubt.

"But?" Scott asked.

Lily hesitated only briefly before she blurted out the message from the archangel. "But first I had to find the House of Prayer."

Scott said nothing as he continued to gaze straight into her eyes.

Lily brushed her hand over the baby's soft curls to hide her agitation. Then she stared at the painting on the opposite wall, a still life depicting a bowl of ruby red pomegranates.

Scott fished around in his pockets for his pipe and tobacco. His expression was blank; revealing nothing Lily could hope to interpret. After what seemed an eternity, he drew a deep puff on the pipe, let the smoke ascend to the ceiling, and then said, "You are welcome to stay as long as you like in the cottage out back. It used to be the caretaker's. It has its own bathroom and a hot plate. Of course, you can come in and use this oversized kitchen anytime you want to."

Lily brushed her lips lightly over the top of Abigail's head. "We both need to get back to Tiberias for a change of clothing."

"And yet?" Scott directed his gaze out the screen door where he could see the cottage. "You seem hesitant."

Lily nodded, took a deep breath, and blurted out, "The archangel has never misled me. I'm positive he said go to the House of Prayer." Lily stared out the open kitchen door into the garden. "Michael didn't say anything about you being here."

Scott's composure did not waver at the mention of the archangel. "I don't know about your message from Michael, but it will be months before any students arrive, if at all. The offer is there. You and your daughter will have all the privacy you need."

Abigail smiled at her mother, and then frowned deeply with an audible grunt. "Ah, I think I will take you up on that offer. My little sweetheart needs to have her diaper changed. You said there's a bathroom out there, hot and cold water?" Lily stood.

"Absolutely," Scott replied as he got up from the table and walked over to a key rack on the opposite wall. "Here's your key. I think you will find everything in order. Shout if you need anything."

Lily soon stood in the open doorway of the cottage. It smelled a bit musty but that could be remedied as soon as she opened the windows. It appeared just as Scott said, a one-room cottage with twin beds, an old-fashioned armoire in the corner, and a more than adequate bathroom that held a large claw-footed bathtub, sink, and toilet. "My darling, let's get you cleaned up."

Later that evening, Lily ate supper with Professor Scott in the big kitchen. Abigail, learning to roll over by herself, played happily on a heavy quilt placed in the middle of the room. Scott got up several times to replenish the dish of olives, pickles, and goat cheese, trying not to look surprised by her appetite as the stack of warm pita disappeared one by one. After taking a big gulp from her glass of water, Lily wiped her mouth with the back of her hand and mumbled, "It's the nursing. I'm always famished."

"Ahh…" He seemed to stumble for a suitable reply. "I know nothing of that."

"I'll do the cooking." She glanced down at her daughter. "As long as we stay here, it's the least I can do to repay your hospitality."

"As I recall, you're not a bad cook." He got up and placed the dirty dishes in the sink. "Washing up is my side of the deal."

* * * *

In the cool evening air, sitting outside in the garden, Lily played with Abigail in her lap. She felt safe sitting in the enclosed garden as Scott proceeded to point out the various neighbors on three sides. "To the left, just over the wall and down one lane is the beginning of the Hassidic neighborhood. Immediately adjacent to us, behind the wall is a Muslim school for girls. Then, to keep it all kosher, so to speak, across from our gate is St. George's School for Boys, Anglican, I believe." He drew in heavily on his pipe, evidently content with the mixed composition of his immediate neighborhood.

Lily allowed herself a small smile. "Just not what I would have expected from Michael."

"You mean the archangel is not known to be ecumenical?"

Lily coughed in embarrassment. "Hardly that, I only meant it is never anything I might have imagined. Like me finding you here in this big old house, and it having a cottage out back, and everything." She quickly bent to resist Abigail's efforts to squirm off her lap. "This little one will soon be crawling."

"I get up at dawn, drink a cup of coffee and leave for the day. You will have the house and garden to yourself."

"Where do you spend your days?" Lily asked,

"City of David excavations. Why? Do you want a private tour?"

Lily hurried to say an emphatic no. "I don't want to go anywhere near the Kidron." She felt her normally tanned face go pale at just the thought of the apparition she had seen behind Absolom's tomb.

Scott stood up. "Well, good night then. You'll have this place all to yourself tomorrow." He added, "There's a gate key hanging in the kitchen in case you want to go out tomorrow. Good night."

"*Lilah tov*, good night professor."

Chapter 14

The unwelcome visitor rang the bell over and over as Ari walked slowly to the gate. He made no move to unlatch it, rather bent to look through the peephole. He saw a mirror image of himself, a man of about the same height and build, but somewhat older, and wearing the black robe favored by Greek Orthodox monks.

It took Ari some moments to recognize his own brother, Reza, impatiently demanding entrance. Surprised but not displeased, he opened the gate, pulled his sibling into the garden with one hand, and then slammed the gate shut again with the other.

The two stood staring shyly at each other. Ari broke the silence. "I didn't expect to see you here." His eyes traveled up and down Reza's garments. "Certainly not dressed like a Greek monk."

A thin smile played across Reza's lips. "It is not the first time I have taken on the persona of a Christian. Last time it was as an Armenian clergyman." Reza shrugged, as if to say it mattered little to him how he dressed. Then he bowed deeply from the waist and took his brother's hand, kissing it in the accepted act of submission.

Ari's demeanor did not change, but he received the token of subservience as his due. "Come, my brother, join me under the grape arbor and tell me what brings you to *El Kuds*, the Holy City." Before Reza could answer, Ari began to boil water in a *finjan* and then made two small cups of hot, sweet coffee. The faint aroma of cardamom drifted above their heads.

Sitting in the shady patio, Reza inquired of Ari's health, and then talked about inconsequential matters, such as tending the garden, asking if he had met his Arab neighbors, and finally, did he get along with the Jews in the archaeological excavations next door. Ari listened patiently, knowing it was the way of Persians to politely circumvent the main subject of a discussion. Eventually, Reza spoke of what brought him to the north side of Mount Zion, to this small and obscure village of Silwan.

"Such a tragic accident." Reza's impassive expression revealed neither sorrow nor regret.

Ari caught his breath and held it. He did not want to talk about the propane explosion which had killed Lily and Abigail. His expression also remained impassive, but inwardly he struggled with emotions that rent his heart to the core. An almost imperceptible tick in his cheek just above the jaw line revealed his inner struggle.

"I choose to remember only the good times," Ari said, resolutely pressing his lips together and saying no more.

"That is wise. Leave the dead to the dead. Face today with renewed effort to bring about your destiny," Reza replied. The bright sunlight diffusing through the grape leaves played on Reza's handsome features, making him appear as if he were a benevolent relative here to console Ari on his unspeakable loss.

After a long period of silence, Reza began to speak, in soft melodious Farsi-accented English, about the Jewish prophet Ezekiel and Zoo-elkareem. "The latter also known as Darius the Great. They were contemporaries, you know, of course."

Not sensing where his brother wanted to go with this history lesson, Ari simply nodded his head, although he did not know these two men of history were contemporaries. In fact, he knew very little about either of them.

Reza continued speaking, his words swelling and peaking like gentle waves in a calm sea. If the subject matter hadn't been so bizarre, Ari might have been lulled into a gentle sleep.

"Gog and Magog will be let loose and will emerge and drink up the Sea of Galilee." Reza paused to take a discreet sip of his coffee, as if his last statement was not extraordinary.

Ari mentally scrambled to make heads or tails of this pronouncement but came up empty. Nothing in his upbringing could have prepared him for this, he ruefully admitted to himself. To hide his growing panic, he also took a sip of coffee hoping the caffeine would calm his spinning thoughts or at least jog his imagination to make some cogent reply.

Not waiting for a response, Reza continued, "And when the Sea of Galilee is dried up, the son of Mary will return." Reza primly wiped the corners of his full lips before setting the coffee cup down.

Ari knew, of course, the reference to the son of Mary could only mean one person, *Yeshua*. How the man from Nazareth fit into this peculiar narrative he did not know, but he did know Reza would soon remind him, in his gentle tutorial manner. And what did he mean about the Sea of Galilee drying up? Like the Dead Sea? Of course, for years the lack of adequate rainfall had depleted the Kinneret fed by the melted snow on Mount Hermon. The water level measured dangerously low but not anywhere near depletion. If this event did occur, which sounded preposterous to Ari's ears, it would mean the end of Israel, as the Sea of Galilee fed by the waters of the Jordan River, was their main water supply.

As the Twelfth Imam, Ari knew he should be familiar with this prophecy about Gog, and what Reza called the other, Magog. But nothing came to his reeling thoughts. Only Yeshua of Nazareth sounded somewhat familiar, yet what this first century Jew had to do with this scenario he could not say.

Ari tried to compose his thoughts, and at the same time keep a sane and knowing expression on his face, as Reza continued speaking. "Volcanoes and flowing magma, Magog. Magma. They are one and the same. The entire area of the Golan Heights above the Sea of Galilee is comprised of ancient volcanic rock."

Ari remembered how he'd had to navigate across the dried lava beds those many years before when he had escaped from the *tekiyah* in Damascus. Is there a prophecy that the volcanoes in the Golan region, which have been dormant for centuries, are about to come violently to life? Did Reza suggest flowing rivers of red-hot magma would surge down the cliffs, obliterating orchards, farms, and kibbutzim with the end result being a boiled dry Sea of Galilee?

"God forbid," slipped involuntarily from Ari's lips. His hand trembled as he took a gulp of his now-cold coffee. He had vowed never to return to the region and town where his beloved wife and child had died. Surely Reza did not intend he should relocate to Tiberias, even though he would be relieved to end this present disguise.

"*Allah Akbar*, God is great," Reza responded automatically to his brother's evocation of the name of the Lord. To Ari's immediate relief, Reza began to speak about Ari's role here in *El Kuds*, the Holy City. "The Jews are determined to rebuild their temple. It is only a matter of time before they create a crisis, and then try to throw us off the Temple Mount, and out of the Al Aksa Mosque.

Our academics are doing everything they can to discredit the Jewish historians and archaeologists who insist they have a long history here."

Ari lifted his eyebrows at this bit of information. How could the Muslims deny three thousand years of history? What about all the recent discoveries in the City of David excavation going on right next door? Only a barbed wired fence separated his garden hideout from the dig. And just yesterday he caught a glimpse of Professor Scott there.

"How's it going, this disinformation campaign?" Ari kept his tone flat but his heart raced as this new information sank in. Would the American academics buy this line? Surely they studied history. But Europe, why not? Anti-Semitism remains in full bloom as the guilt of the Holocaust recedes in the memory of most Europeans. With a sick feeling in the pit of his stomach, Ari began to regret he'd aligned himself with this culture of dissimulation and lies. He thought back to that night on the Sea of Galilee with his fishing partner. What had Shimon said? Ari could be Israel's Trojan horse. With the pain of his wife's and daughter's deaths sitting on his heart like a closed fist, he felt his resolve ebb away. He no longer wanted to be, or even to pretend to be this Mahdi. Bitter bile burned the back of his throat. To hide his wretched state of mind from his brother, he went to the cupboard and pored himself a cool glass of water from a clay jug.

Reza calmly brushed a piece of lint off his black robe, and continued his account of how the public relations war between the two cultures should play out. According to his highly placed sources, the Mahdi Brotherhood had it under control and moved the necessary people around with the skill of master chess players.

Chapter 15

The next morning after Reza's departure, Ari needed to find some answers. He made up his mind to consult with the only two people in Israel he could trust. He knew from past experience they would have his best interests at heart and, more importantly, they had known Lily and would be sympathetic if he wanted to talk about his dead wife and child.

After his morning ablutions, he gazed in disgust at his monk's robe. With a determination that surprised him, he tossed the hated garment on the floor, and pulled on his old pair of jeans and a not-so-clean undershirt. Looking in the little mirror over the sink, he grimaced at the sight of his unruly curls. Today he would not pull his hair back and tie it neatly at the back of his neck. With a quick shake of his head, his curly hair tumbled around his face with abandon. His lips turned down in a sardonic smile as he recognized the image—a regular Israeli worker.

Skipping his normal cup of coffee, Ari left the Greek Orthodox garden without so much as a backward glance. He walked down the narrow lane that led out onto the main street of the Silwan neighborhood passing a few early risers. In front of the Dung Gate, he noted a group of Orthodox men walking to the Western Wall for their morning prayer. A distant church bell rang from the nearby Mount of Olives. The pale yellow sun climbed over the Judean hills, and for a short time the predawn dew sparkled on the sparse roadside vegetation. By midmorning Ari knew the intense rays would beat down mercilessly on humans and vegetation without partiality.

Taking the path outside the wall, it took only ten minutes to reach Zion Gate. Here he entered into the Armenian Quarter of the Old City, walking quickly with his head down, not that he expected to be recognized by anyone. He didn't think about the brothers, Dan and Eli, not being at home at this hour. It never occurred to him they might be on a trip, or visiting their elderly mother in Tel Aviv. Like a man possessed, he strode determinedly to their apartment above the tailor shop. Standing in front of their iron gate, he vigorously rang the bell.

After a few tense moments, a voice drifted down from a second story window. "*Mi Zeh*? Who is it?"

Ari looked up into the annoyed face of his friend Dan. "It's me, Ari. Let me in, I need to talk to you." Ari shrugged at the puzzled look on Dan's face.

"I'll be right down. Give me a minute to get dressed." Dan spoke quietly so as not to attract attention from his Christian neighbors. Not many Jews chose to live in this quarter of the city, where outsiders were not welcome, even if they professed to be Messianic Christians. Dan and his brother Eli were loners and long since reconciled to their solitary status.

The green metal gate opened, and Dan offered his hand in a warm welcome. "*Barukh ha ba*, welcome," he said by way of greeting to his early morning visitor. "What brings you to us at this hour?"

Ari stepped inside the courtyard and accepted the outstretched hand, and then surprised himself by embracing Dan in a warm bear hug. Unbidden tears filled his eyes as he remembered his previous stay here with Lily. He wondered if the brothers had heard about the gas explosion in Tiberias. Recovering his composure, he followed Dan up the staircase to their apartment.

Eli crossed from the kitchen area to the living room carrying a pot of freshly brewed coffee. With a big smile on his face, he told Ari to take a seat on the low sofa. "Let's have our first cup before anything else."

"*Tov*, good." Ari gratefully sipped the rich Viennese-style brew.

After a suitable time, Eli took the initiative and asked Ari what was so urgent he needed to talk to them at the crack of dawn. "Not that it's an imposition. You know our routine; we are at prayer before the birds begin to sing."

Ari stared into his now-empty cup, and then looked around the sparsely but tastefully furnished room. Nothing had changed. He could trust them, he reminded himself. *But where should I begin — the Mount of Olives, Mt. Sinai, the Greek garden next to the City of David*? He bit his lips. *Should I start with deaths of my wife and daughter*?

In the pause, Dan tried to fill the awkward silence. "We spoke to Lily only a few days ago." Dan appeared to be carefully considering his choice of words now. "She seemed extremely anxious about your whereabouts."

The stricken look on Ari's face caused Eli to add. "We don't want to meddle in your personal affairs, but she did appear to be upset. We hardly knew what to say."

Ari pressed his palm to his forehead, as if in pain. The brothers looked at each other and shrugged helplessly.

Staring at them, Ari spoke in a tight, measured voice, "Then you haven't heard the news?"

"News, well no, we don't get a daily paper, but we do listen to Kol Israel every evening." Eli frowned and continued. "We're not totally out of touch."

"They're gone." Ari mumbled, now gazing at the stone floor.

"Who's gone? You mean Lily left you?" Dan shook his head in disbelief.

Eli spoke up, "They were here in Jerusalem, looking for you."

Not able to contain himself, Ari abruptly stood up and paced around the room like a wild man. "No, no, they're gone, a gas explosion in Tiberias." He waved his arms, looking from one to the other. "Do I have to say the word, dead?" His shoulders hunched as he began to weep openly.

Dan and Eli turned towards each other with a stunned expression on their faces. Then Eli asked, "It's not possible. We talked to her at Christ Church only recently."

"Oh no, it's true. I read it in the paper." Ari wiped the tears away and with effort composed his features.

"Don't believe everything you read in the newspapers," Dan added. "Come sit down, Ari. We have to get to the bottom of this." He motioned for Ari to take his seat again. "You're convinced they're dead, and we're certain it's not true."

Eli pressed his hands together in his lap to compose his thoughts. "Don't you have a high-level contact in the Mossad? We seem to remember you telling us something about a fellow called Pincus."

"Yeah, this Pincus kept you and Lily under constant surveillance, right?"

Ari's black eyebrows knitted together in one continuous line as he thought this over. "Yes, Agent Pincus was an unwelcome shadow."

"Well, there you go. Speak with him today. He can tell you where Lily is."

"I know where Lily is," Ari growled.

"Just for the sake of argument, let's assume none of us knows the real story. It can't hurt to talk to him."

Ari slowly shook his head. "You don't know where I've been these last weeks. I nearly went over to the other side." He rubbed his chin thoughtfully. "No, to be honest, I did go over to their side."

"Whose side?" Eli asked.

"The Mahdi Brotherhood's side."

The two brothers exchanged a knowing glance.

Ari continued, "I've spent time on the backside of the Mount of Olives, and then they took me to the Sinai. At the monastery there, I met my half-brother Reza again." He looked up at his two friends, and decided to tell them everything, all but the bizarre earthquake scenario Reza had spoken about. "The time has come for the Holy One, the hidden Mahdi, to be revealed."

"And you think that is you?" Dan asked in a surprised tone as he looked toward his brother for help.

Eli stood with hands outstretched in supplication. "Ari, don't be deceived. You are not their messiah. Don't believe their lies."

Ari bent his head with his hands covering his eyes. "Oh God, how did I get into this mess."

"It's mind control. Besides that, they kidnapped you. Remember? You were not a willing participant."

"Well, yes," Ari replied hesitantly.

Eli continued, "I still think you should visit Pincus as soon as possible. Get the facts about your family."

At the mention of his wife and daughter, Ari turned, not wanting them to see his pain. "I'll go to his office, now."

* * * *

An hour after Ari left the apartment in the Armenian Quarter; Lily stood before the same green metal gate and rang the bell.

Eli stuck his head out the window over the archway, and Lily saw his eyes widen in surprise as he recognized her. "I'll be right down," he shouted.

With all speed, Lily and Abigail were hustled upstairs and seated at the kitchen table. Lily accepted a cup of milky coffee and was avidly buttering a roll when she stopped, hand in midair. "Why are you so delighted to see me? Your face shows it."

"You tell her." Dan glanced at his brother.

"Come on, let's hear it," Lily said, with her mouth half full. Eli hesitated, and pulled on the sleeve of his cotton sweater. "You guys are the only people I know who wear sweaters in the summer." Lily smiled indulgently at her friends.

"First, tell us why you're here this morning," Dan said, obviously not wanting to reveal too much.

Lily lifted one shoulder in the typical Middle Eastern way that implied—*why not*. Then and there, she decided to tell the brothers about her message from the archangel Michael. She described in detail the concert rehearsal at the YMCA, then finding Professor Scott, quite by happenstance, who then offered her a place to stay while she waited for Ari to return. "God only knows where he is." She sighed audibly.

Abigail began to squirm in her sling, indicating she wanted room to kick her chubby legs and roll about. "All right with you guys if I put her down on the rug?" She looked from one to the other. Without waiting for their permission she lowered the baby to the camel hair carpet.

"What's the matter? Come on, I can see it in your eyes. You're dying to tell me something." Lily straightened up as she put her hand on her lower back to ease the strain of carrying Abigail.

"Why don't you sit down again?" Eli motioned to the chair at the breakfast table. He in turn took his seat, and poured another round. Dan followed his brother's lead, sat down and spooned sugar in his coffee, stirring vigorously.

Lily quietly folded her hands. "I came here to get your input about this House of Prayer. Of course, it's not called that now. It belongs to Scott's university, and will be used as a dig house for his student interns. But what the heck, I can stay there in the meantime." She looked up and took another breath. "I'm just babbling away. I don't know what I want to say."

The only noise in the room was the soft coos and squeals coming from where Abigail entertained herself on the carpet.

Eli loudly cleared his throat. "I find it curious Michael directed you to the professor's dig house. I remember that property when the Baptists owned it. Over in East Jerusalem, right?"

"Yes, across from Saint George's," Lily answered.

"My brother and I don't know much about this professor. Where did you say he works?"

Lily brushed some crumbs off her fingers. "He's working at the City of David excavation."

"Ah." Eli glanced at his brother, as if to confirm they were both thinking the same thing. "Do you remember us talking with you about the restoration of the fallen tabernacle of David?"

"Yes, of course I remember," Lily said. "But are you saying those archaeologists are a part of your group?"

Dan quickly responded, "No, Lily, we have nothing to do with this excavation or the people working there. But it's not coincidental you are now connected, however vaguely, with the City of David. That's all I'm saying."

Stalling for time to compose her thoughts, Lily smoothed the wrinkles out of her skirt. "I seem to remember you once said Ari was also a part of this restoration."

"Yes, and speaking of Ari, we have some news." Dan paused for dramatic effect.

Lily's hand rose to her mouth. "Has something happened to him?"

"He's fine," Dan replied. "At least physically. We are concerned about his mental state, though."

"What do you mean? Have you seen him?" Lily's voice rose in agitation, causing Abigail to cry. She quickly bent down, picked up her child, and held her tightly in her arms. "There, there," she murmured softly. "I didn't mean to upset you darling."

Taking charge, Eli led Lily and the baby to the sitting room sofa. "Ari is fine. He came here this morning. Right now he's at Agent Pincus's office trying to find out what happened to you."

"Me?" Lily asked, sounding incredulous.

"He thinks you two died in a gas explosion in Tiberias. He read about it in the paper."

Lily shook her head in confusion. "I don't read newspapers. Or even listen to the nightly news. You say reports of my death?" Her arm instinctively cradled Abigail. "You told him you saw us recently, didn't you?"

"Yes, but he didn't believe us. That's why we suggested he get the facts from Pincus." Eli adjusted his glasses, taking them off, wiping them on his sleeve and putting them back on. "Also, he confided to us he has turned his back on this Mahdi Brotherhood business." He looked hard at Lily as if to assess her reaction.

"Is that where he has been these past weeks? With Reza?" Lily felt the blood drain out of her face.

Dan broke in gently, "We'll leave it to Ari to tell you about where he's been." He then patted Lily awkwardly on the shoulder. "After he talks to Pincus, I'm pretty sure he'll return here."

Lily cuddled Abigail and murmured. "Abba will be here soon, *motek*."

Chapter 16

The Mossad offices took up two floors of a nondescript building off Jaffa road, not far from the Russian Compound. Motti Pincus sat at a desk piled high with folders and reports. His eyes scanned each page with practiced speed and accuracy, looking for the chance word, or the anomaly. Sometimes he would cease reading, and make a notation in his small neat Hebrew script. He had asked his assistant to give him all the files they had on the civilian company made up of former intelligence members that spoke not only Arabic, but also Farsi. A slender file labeled *Terrogence* lay open before him.

He read a concise profile on Ari's half-brother, Reza. He was last spotted on the Island of Kish in the Persian Gulf. This Reza fellow had a meeting with a high-ranking cleric from Mecca. Pincus knew the ayatollahs in Iran were diametrically opposed to the doctrine of their counterparts in Mecca. The Sunni/Shi'ite rivalry did not bode well for Israel. On the issue of the hated Zionist, these religious clerics would find agreement.

Pincus took off his glasses and rubbed his eyes. His tea, now cold, sat before him. He rang the buzzer that would signal housekeeping to bring him another hot glass filled with fresh *nanna*. The old-fashioned phone on his desk rang shrilly. He put his glasses on as if that would help his hearing. "Yes, escort him up immediately."

Pincus methodically and thoroughly cleared his desk of files and papers, starting with the *Terrogence* file, which he placed in a locked drawer. By the time his unexpected visitor arrived, the desktop held nothing but a notepad and several pens. Pincus's posture and demeanor arranged itself in a position he hoped would look like relaxed indifference.

When the office door opened Pincus allowed himself a small smile not entirely counterfeit. He liked Ari Ben Chaim, but at the same time did not entirely trust him. How had they recently lost all trace of Ari? Where had he learned his tradecraft? Too many questions left unanswered. Pincus nevertheless felt relieved to have Ari in his office.

"*Barukh ha ba*, welcome," Pincus said, adding, "Tea or coffee?"

Ari sat stiffly in the straight-backed chair opposite the desk. He maintained a stone-faced demeanor as he shook his head to the offer of refreshment. The agent who brought him to the office nodded to Pincus, and silently left the room. Weak sunlight streamed in through the streaked windows that opened onto a balcony.

Pincus leaned back in his swivel chair and spoke in what he assumed to be an affable tone. "Why am I honored with your presence this morning?" It being a rhetorical question, he did not wait for Ari to answer. "You know we've been scouring the earth for you. And I must say your ability to stay under our radar is remarkable. In fact, you could give our boys some lessons, if you would ever like to help our side."

Ari shrugged. "Our side? Aren't we on the same side?"

"I thought we were." Pincus focused his attention on his long, freckled fingers. "I thought we had an understanding to keep in touch."

Ari didn't respond to the implied accusation. "What about Lily and Abigail's deaths?" He flung the words in Pincus's face with the force of a hand grenade.

Pincus looked momentarily startled. "Death? How much do you know?"

"Only what I read in the paper," Ari retorted. "And what my brother Reza told me."

"Reza, you've seen him recently? He's in Israel?" Pincus immediately regretted his error in revealing the Mossad did not know this fact.

"Never mind Reza, I demand some answers." Ari glowered at Pincus. "I've just learned my wife and daughter didn't die as reported. In fact, they are very much alive!" Ari took a big gulp of air to steady his nerves.

Pincus fiddled with the pen on the desk. "Oh, and who gave you this *intel*?"

"It doesn't matter who. Is it true?"

Pincus noted the anguish in Ari's demeanor and voice. He hated to drag this out any longer than necessary, but at the same time he wanted to elicit useful intelligence from Ari while he was in this state of agitation. "Give me the name of your source, and I'll tell you if it's true or not." Pincus's eyes were now hard and flat as he morphed into this well-practiced bargaining mode.

Ari sadly shook his head. "You already have a file on Dan and Eli and you know they're not a threat. They told me Lily is alive, and you could confirm it." He stared directly at Pincus. "I'm not leaving this office until I know the facts."

Pincus could tell Ari grieved deeply for his wife and child. He felt he had pushed the poor man as far as he could and was satisfied with the results. "They're both alive," Pincus said gently.

Ari sat absolutely still. Only the tears streaking down his cheeks revealed the depth of his emotions. Pincus looked away in respect for Ari's dignity. A long moment passed as Ari composed himself enough to sufficiently ask the next pertinent detail. "Where are they now? I want to see them."

Pincus picked up his desk phone and punched in some numbers. After a moment, he spoke to someone on the other end. "My colleague will be able to give us an updated report." He put the phone back in its cradle. "While we wait for him, let me ask housekeeping to bring you some tea."

Ari's voice sounded hoarse, as he responded with a simple, "*Toda*, thanks." It was not long before someone brought in two glasses, placed them on the desk and left. Then a young agent entered the office, and placed a typed report in front of Pincus.

"Ari, meet Benny. He is assigned to keep a day and night watch on your wife and daughter."

Ari half stood and shook the man's hand with no small amount of hostility mixed with gratitude. "Right, let's get on with it," Ari said gruffly.

The junior agent looked to his superior for direction. "Tell him all you know about Lily's whereabouts, Benny," Pincus said.

Looking doubtful, Benny hesitated a long moment.

"Get on with it, man. Ari is on our side," Pincus added.

"Well, we followed Giverette Ben Chaim and her child from Tiberias to Christ Church Hostel. She met an archaeologist, by the name of Eugene Scott, who took her on a little *tiyul* to Wadi Kidron." He stopped the narrative there, as if weighing what to leave in and what to keep out of his account. Evidently thinking it prudent to leave nothing out, he added, "Something in the *wadi*, above or near Absolom's Tomb, spooked Lily and she has not gone back there." Pincus raised his eyebrows, but nodded for Benny to continue. "The next day, she left Christ Church and had breakfast at the King David Hotel. I then followed her to a place in East Jerusalem where she again met with Professor Scott. Whether this was prearranged, I don't know. She spent the night there." He looked casually at Ari to gauge his response to this bit of information. Seeing no reaction on his face, he continued his narrative. "This morning, she walked from this house, a mansion I would call it, and arrived at an apartment in the Armenian Quarter. According to my records, two Jewish brothers, originally from New York live there." He looked up, first at Pincus and then at Ari. "That's it."

"She's at Dan and Eli's?" Ari jumped to his feet knocking over his glass causing the agent Benny to step back to avoid being splashed.

"I've got a watch on the lane. If they leave, I'll be notified." Benny sounded miffed, as if Ari thought he couldn't handle the job of watching one woman and her child.

Reaching for the door, Ari turned and leaned heavily against the doorframe, his head bent.

"Steady on." Pincus nodded to Benny. "Escort our guest out of the building."

Chapter 17

Ari ran down the narrow alley that led to Jaffa Road, dashed through the intersection against a red light, and caused a bus driver to suddenly hit the brakes. The irate driver hurled imprecations at Ari while his shaken passengers tried to regain their dignity.

Just before reaching Jaffa Gate Ari slowed down to a brisk walk, well aware anybody running like a madman would attract the attention of the Border Patrol. The municipality was still renovating the square inside the gate, and pedestrians were obliged to keep to the crowded, narrow sidewalk. A group of tourists ambled at their leisure before him, blocking his attempts to pick up speed. Finally the group, Scandinavians by the looks of them, angled off down the steps to King David Street, leaving Ari free to walk with long strides to the lane which led to Dan and Eli's apartment.

His heart pounded, not only from the frantic exertion, but also from the hope he would find his beloved Lily and darling Abigail waiting there. Was the Mossad ever wrong? A shadow crossed his mind like a bad omen. Of course, Pincus could be wrong. They received bad or garbled intelligence. He desperately wanted to believe, and therefore would give Pincus the benefit of a doubt.

Standing in front of the familiar green metal gate, he looked up at the window over the archway. Heartsick with longing, he half expected to see Lily's smiling face there. He squared his shoulders and forcefully rang the bell to the apartment. Looking up, he saw Dan appear at the second floor window.

After what felt like an eternity, but was in fact less than a minute, the gate opened. Dan stood there with a silly grin on his face. "Come in, Ari, we've been waiting for you."

Ari's expression froze in undisguised surprise. Sensing his emotions were about to spiral out of control, he forcibly steadied his nerves, took a deep breath and slowly exhaled.

The levity left Dan's face as he stared at Ari's strained expression. "Come upstairs. They're anxious to see you."

Ari forced back the tears that threatened to overwhelm him. "Not as anxious as I am." Bounding ahead, he took the steps two at a time. When he reached the landing, he saw Lily reaching out to embrace him. They fell in each other's arms crying and murmuring words Dan could not distinguish but could imagine. "Come in, we don't want the neighbors gossiping."

Once inside, Ari didn't want to let go of his wife, but Lily broke away from his embrace to motion towards Abigail, happily crawling on the carpet. "Abba is here, darling."

Ari knelt down and picked up his daughter, inhaling her milky scent as he planted kisses in the folds of her neck and round cheeks. "My little dove, you're alive." His voice broke and he could say no more as he rocked to and fro.

Dan and Eli beamed at each other and then turned to leave the room.

"Wait. You don't have to go," Lily said, as she wiped her wet cheeks with the back of her hand. "We can go to the cottage where I'm staying and have all the privacy we want." She turned to Ari. "Scott has allowed me to stay on his property."

Ari gazed at Lily with fond amusement. "*Beseder*, all right, lead the way." He placed Abigail into the crook of one arm, and then offered Lily his other as they left the apartment in the Armenian Quarter.

Twenty minutes later, hidden behind the high walls of Professor Scott's compound, Ari and Lily sat in the cottage. Lily spooned yoghurt, mixed with a mashed banana, into Abigail's wide open mouth.

"Like feeding a fat, baby dove," Ari said, feasting his eyes on the two people he loved more than anything in the world. "Abby has grown so big."

"Yes, I'll soon replace her baby sling for a backpack-style carrier," Lily replied, as she wiped the dribble off Abigail's chin with a kitchen towel. "I'm looking forward to you doing most of the schlepping from now on."

"I desire nothing more," Ari replied. They continued to exchange pleasant conversation as if the recent events had never occurred. Ari did not feel ready to bring up the subject of his time spent on Mt. Sinai with his brother Reza, or his solitary hideaway in the Greek garden. Neither did Lily appear eager to talk about the harrowing vision she had seen on her walk with Professor Scott.

Lily finished feeding Abigail, changed her diapers, and then laid her down for a nap on the twin bed against the wall. She carefully arranged pillows to keep the baby from rolling off the bed in her sleep.

Ari put his arms around Lily and pulled her close, crushing her to his chest. Their lips met in a warm, slow kiss as they tumbled almost in slow motion down onto the other twin bed. The gentle sound of their love blended with the doves softly cooing in the crevices of the tile roof over them. Sweet sleep came to all three of them as the afternoon wore away.

* * * *

The laughter of children drifted over the garden wall which separated them from the school next door. The noise caused Lily to open her eyes and glance over at Abigail who began to stir after her nap. "Here, my darling, come drink." She lifted her daughter up to nurse.

Ari stirred, and then raised his head as she rearranged the pillows at his back. "Not a bad place you have here. Better than where I've been living."

Lily looked at him with a scowl on her face. "And just where has that been? I've been frantic with worry, you know."

Ari looked guilty. "Lily darling, it has been a wild journey. I hardly know where to begin." Before he could continue, he heard a rap at the door and stopped cold. Putting a finger to his lips, he motioned to Lily to get dressed, as he quickly slipped on his trousers and crawled to the window.

"Lily, I have fixings for dinner. Do you still want to cook tonight?" Scott called through the closed door.

Ari shrugged in embarrassment then opened the door.

"My word, the prodigal son has returned." Scott stared at Ari.

Neither Ari nor Lily recognized his biblical reference to a prodigal son, but they both understood he meant Ari's unexpected appearance. Ari took the professor's hand and shook it warmly. "I'm indebted to you for offering my family a place to stay."

"My pleasure," Scott replied heartedly. "Just think of it as repaying the hospitality you showed me in Ain Karem."

Lily quickly broke in, "I'm ready to prepare dinner. What do you have?" As if in mutual agreement, all questions would be put off to a later time. Together they entered the mansion by the back door and went directly into the large kitchen. Lily handed Abby to Ari and began to prepare the mountain of vegetables spread on the counter top. Before long, the fragrant aroma of ratatouille simmered on the stovetop. She sliced a crusty loaf of bread, put out an array of pickles, olives, cucumbers, and tomatoes, and then sat down to take a break. "How about some more lemonade, if you have any left?" Lily asked.

Scott smiled. "What can I say? This is indeed a most pleasant surprise." Glancing casually in Ari's direction, he added, "Where have you been all this time, if I may be so bold as to ask?"

"You don't really want to know," Ari replied.

"All right," Scott replied, his face expressionless. "I can respect your need for privacy." He picked up a black olive, put it in his mouth and savored it before spitting the pit into his hand. "My offer to Lily still stands. The back cottage is available as long as she needs it, and that includes you."

Lily put down the bread knife, and focused her attention on Ari. The only sounds in the kitchen were Abigail's babble. Their future together as a family hung on the fragile thread of his response.

Ari leaned forward and took Lily's hand in his. "I don't ever want to be separated again." His voice caught, and then in a moment he continued, "I've lived for so long believing you were dead, blaming myself. Now, I've been given a second chance." He looked directly into Lily's eyes, now overflowing with tears.

Chapter 18

Reza hid in the shadow of a flowering jacaranda tree across the street from the mansion. Behind him, he heard the sounds of a soccer game in progress at St. George's School for Boys. He lingered there as long as he dared, hoping Ari or Lily would appear through the double metal gates. He knew his eyes had not deceived him, but he needed to verify that the she-devil Lily and her miserable spawn were alive and well. "Somebody will pay the ultimate penalty for this mistake," he muttered, his words hanging in the sultry air.

The gate to the school opened, and two teenage boys wearing white shirts and black trousers nodded in his direction. "Good evening, Father," they said in unison.

Reza's eyes widened in surprise, and his shoulders tensed until he remembered he was still dressed in the robe and hat of a Greek Orthodox cleric. He nodded sourly in their direction as they hurried off, eager to escape the confines of their school.

Knowing he risked drawing attention to himself if he stood there any longer, he walked at a brisk pace in the direction of the American Colony Hotel. In the courtyard of the hotel, he faded into the colorful mosaic of Arab men and foreign journalists.

A bellhop pocketed Reza's tip with a smile of satisfaction. "How can I assist you?"

Reza affably replied, "I am just passing through the neighborhood, and I find I need some refreshment." He took a white handkerchief out of his sleeve and wiped his brow.

The bellhop nodded knowingly. "The café is inside."

Without further comment, Reza entered the sprawling old hotel. His eyes blinked as they adjusted to the dim interior with its bubbling fountain and ornate blue tiles. He found a seat at a small table for one and glanced around to see if his presence caused any undue notice. Most of the hotel guests sat or stood on the other side of the lobby, where they were evidently imbibing alcohol. No one even looked in his direction.

In this quiet moment of respite from the heat, Reza found himself perplexed, and not for the first time, by the actions of his half-brother. Why did Ari now dress as an ordinary Israeli? And how did his wife and child, who by all accounts had burned to death in a gas explosion, accompany him? Things were definitely not going according to plan.

Eventually a waiter appeared and took his order. Some minutes later, Reza delicately sipped his glass of mint tea and felt his blood start to cool. Again, his thoughts turned to his half-brother. Would Ari remain with his family or return to the Greek-owned garden? Considerable effort had been required to secure that garden safe house. Did his brother appreciate all he'd done for him? Reza weighed the evidence and came to the bitter conclusion that Lily was not only alive, but also reunited with her husband. In which case, Ari could not continue in the guise of a Greek Orthodox monk. Therefore, Reza would also be obliged to change his own disguise. A thin smile curved his lips as he contemplated shedding the uncomfortable black tunic and tall hat. New arrangements would have to be made, and he looked forward to the challenge this presented.

Reza's meditations were abruptly interrupted by the unexpected appearance of the concierge of the hotel. "Begging your indulgence, sir," The man said in an obsequious tone, "I have a message for you." The man placed a small, white envelope on the table by the empty tea glass.

Reza nodded in acknowledgment as the concierge backed away. His pulse raced with apprehension. No one knew he would be here. It was a spontaneous decision he now regretted making. Who could possibly have sent him a message? He casually tapped his slender fingers on the table but did not pick up the envelope. He stared directly ahead, and then slowly glanced over his left shoulder to the entrance and observed a thin Arab man in a wrinkled linen suit exiting the hotel lobby.

Reza then looked toward the group of men in the cocktail lounge. They looked like bored foreign journalists of one nationality or another amusing themselves as they waited for some action between the Arabs and the Jews. No one paid the slightest attention to the Greek Orthodox cleric having tea on the other side of the room.

Reza hesitantly picked up the envelope with the tips of his fingers, wrinkling his nose as if the message had a bad smell. He slit the seal with his thumb and slid out a thin sheet of paper. Putting on his reading glasses, he read: "Fatimah sends her regards. Meet me in the bookshop at five p.m."

Reza slipped the note in the pocket of his robe and glanced at his watch. After gently dabbing with a paper tissue at the moisture that suddenly appeared on his upper lip, he signaled the waiter to bring him another glass of mint tea.

Precisely at five, Reza placed money on the table and casually walked out the entrance of the hotel. In a corner of the courtyard, he located the bookstore. A small placard in the window announced this was the largest English language bookstore in the Middle East. "What an overstatement," Reza mumbled to himself. "This is probably the *only* English bookshop in the whole region."

Nevertheless, he straightened his back and put on a serious demeanor. Then his eyes fell on the old-fashioned copper house key placed in a corner of the window. This secret symbol assured him that he had indeed been summoned to rendezvous with a member of the Mahdi Brotherhood.

A bell tinkling overhead announced his arrival. The same man he had seen dressed in the rumpled linen suit came forward to greet him. Reza assumed him to be the proprietor.

"Fatimah sends her respects." Reza spoke the code words in English rather than Farsi or Arabic.

"Ali responds in kind," responded the bookshop owner, also in English. "Please, follow me to my private office in the back."

Reza sniffed delicately as the odor of dust mingled with a touch of mildew hit his nostrils. It was not a familiar scent, but neither was it offensive. He assumed that so many books crammed into such a small area produced this effect. *Who comes here and actually buys books?*

The man in the linen suit introduced himself as Yusef, the owner of the bookstore. As if in answer to Reza's unspoken question, he said, "Most of my customers are expatriates, or English speaking Jews."

"No matter," Reza assured him with a half-smile. "Look at me impersonating a Christian. Anything to stay under the radar."

"Of course, of course." Yusef hastened to pull out a chair for Reza. Only after his guest sat down did he take his own seat behind his desk. "May I offer you cold water?"

Reza dismissed the thought of refreshments with a slight wave of his hand. He leaned forward, unable to relax his guard until he ascertained how Yusef knew he would be at the American Colony Hotel today. "Why have you summoned me?"

Yusef took out a delicate, cambric handkerchief and wiped the back of his neck. "I recognized you in the café, and naturally assumed you came to the American Colony to contact me." He then added, "Forgive my presumption, your Excellency. A member of the Brotherhood has never visited my bookstore before this day. I, of course, occasionally attend secret gatherings with fellow members, and we have discussed the Persian who is a blood relative of the Mahdi. We even debated among ourselves why the Holy One and his brother would choose to disguise themselves as Greek Orthodox monks."

Reza furrowed his black brows at learning his presence in Jerusalem had been so openly known. "My disguise does not concern you," he curtly responded.

The bookstore owner began to sweat profusely as his face paled. "When I saw you sitting in the café, I naturally assumed you were here to see me. Please except my humble apologies if I have presumed too much."

Reza felt an immediate sense of relief, but too canny to reveal his state of mind to a subordinate, he looked sternly at the man sitting behind the desk. Learning he had not been followed, nor had the bookshop owner been expecting him, Reza could safely formulate a new plan of action. The first thing he must do is get rid of his religious garb. And he would use the services of this good man to accomplish this task.

"You have not overstepped your place. Calm yourself on that point," Reza said magnanimously. Reza noted the relief on Yusef's face. The benefits of being closely related to the Holy One were not lost on him. Reza continued, "I will need a room here at the hotel for an indeterminate number of days." Without waiting for a response, he added, "I will also need a complete change of apparel." Reza pinched the black wool of his robe in his delicate fingers. "I want you to arrange to have a tailor come to my room tomorrow morning."

The bookseller's relief was palpable. He smiled broadly, revealing an abundance of good teeth which contrasted with his tan complexion. "I can arrange the best suite in the hotel immediately. Finding a discrete tailor on such short notice will not be easy, but it is doable."

With deft fingers he dialed his mobile phone. After a few pleasantries back and forth, Yusef booked a secluded suite. "It is in the name of my brother-in-law. He has recently arrived from Amman. You will have complete privacy when the tailor arrives tomorrow to measure you for new garments."

* * * *

Later that week, Reza in his smartly tailored suit, looked like the other Middle Eastern businessmen that frequented the American Colony Hotel. Though he never drank alcohol at the popular bar, he was often seen sipping a glass of soda and lime. Late at night, visitors came and went from his suite situated off a secluded courtyard. Waiters and bellhops, under the pay of security personnel from various nations, faithfully reported on the goings and comings. Reza remained serene and confident, a man biding his time, who knows events will take place at the set time.

By the third week of his stay in East Jerusalem, it became apparent he must initiate contact with his brother, the Mahdi, and not the other way around as he had hoped. They were living within a half-mile of each other, but it could have been a continent apart for all the chance that they would meet by accident. To accomplish this aim of a meeting, Reza sent the bookstore owner to hand deliver a written invitation to Ari.

Chapter 19

Ari woke before the others, inhaling the fragrance of a well-tended garden wafting in the open window. The heady smell of roses reminded him of his earliest years on the kibbutz. Enough time had passed to heal the raw pain of his parents' brutal deaths, and he could now think about Moshe and Shifra, the only parents he had ever known, without the desire for revenge. He sat up and rested on one arm as he looked with fondness at Lily, still sleeping and gently snoring at his side.

When Abigail began to stir in the other twin bed, he slipped out of the covers, pulled on his jeans, and picked her up before she woke Lily. "Good morning, *motek*, my little sweetie." With the baby in his arms, he went out into the garden, the dew tickling the bottom of his bare feet as he walked across the grass. "Let's pick some roses for *Imma*, shall we?"

Again, the luscious blossoms in the rose garden reminded him of his kibbutz, with attar of roses having been their main market product. He had been three years old when Moshe and Shifra took him from the orphanage in Jerusalem. He could not conjure up any memories before the eventful day of his adoption. But as an adult, he had learned a nurse at the Baby Home, as orphanages of that period where called, had shown him partiality, showering him with abundant affection and attention. She too had been murdered, back in her hometown in England. Evidently there were no lengths to which the Mahdi Brotherhood would not go to advance the Holy One's mission.

Ari hugged his daughter tightly in his arms as these old memories swept unbidden through his mind. "I will protect you with my life, my little daughter." He shook his head, as if to clear it of cobwebs. *What compelled me to contact the Brotherhood again? How stupid and yes, how conceited I am.*

He blushed with shame and remorse for having put his wife and daughter through this recent ordeal. Grateful that no one could see his face he bent down and gently sat Abigail on the grass. He took his pocketknife and began to gather a luscious bouquet of roses. Abigail could now not only sit, but also quickly went on her hands and knees to explore the garden. She hadn't gone far before she stopped to watch a caterpillar inch its way across the grass. She reached for it, but her pudgy fingers failed to grasp it.

Suddenly, Lily appeared running across the courtyard, her white nightgown billowing out behind her. "Ari, what are you doing?" Fear and reproach made her voice sound sharper than she intended.

At the sound of her approaching footsteps, before he heard her voice, Ari spun around, the open blade of his knife perfectly balanced in his right hand, his left arm raised to ward off an attacker. His pulse quickened to the deadly beat that spelled catastrophe to his intended target. His eyes narrowed to cold, hard slits as he scanned the landscape, even as he half crouched, perfectly balancing from foot to foot.

Lily swooped up Abigail into her arms, then stood and gazed at her husband with a strange look on her face. "You can't take your eyes off her. She puts everything she finds in her mouth now."

"Sorry." Ari folded the knife and stuck it in his back pocket. "But you don't need to look so shocked. I only want to protect the two of you."

Lily put her other arm around her husband. "Of course, darling, I know. But we're safe here." She looked up at the high wall that surrounded the property on every side.

With a sheepish expression, Ari pushed a handful of cut roses at Lily. "I intended to put these on your pillow."

Before she could respond, they both looked up as Professor Scott approached them coming from the direction of the back door of the big house. Not knowing how much he might have seen, they moved apart and strode towards him.

"All of you up so early." Scott gave them a big smile. "I thought only we archaeologists were up and about just after daybreak." Not giving them a chance to respond, he added, "Come, I have a big pot of coffee on the stove, plus a mountain of buttered toast."

Lily patted her hair, trying to tame the unruly strands. "Let me take Abigail back to our cottage." She glanced at Ari before continuing, "I'll put on some proper clothes and change her diaper."

"You sure you don't need help?" Ari said, sounding contrite.

Scott took his arm and propelled him to the kitchen door. "Lily will be along. But first, you and I need to talk."

Ari leaned against a counter with his arms folded across his chest. "I'm guessing you saw me waving a knife about."

"I did." Scott poured fragrant coffee into two cups. "Sugar or milk?"

"Both," Ari replied tersely.

"Let's sit." Scott pulled a chair out from the table. "I know you two are once again in some kind of trouble. The Shin Bet people don't follow just anybody. I happened to bump into Lily here in Jerusalem, and I don't need to tell you she's been driven to distraction by your absence."

Ari cupped the fresh coffee in both hands then took a sip. He knew Scott could be trusted to keep a secret. That wasn't the immediate concern. How far did he want Scott to get involved? Would the Brotherhood murder him, like they had the others? Just staying here in the back cottage put Scott in jeopardy, although nobody knew they had spent a night here. Or did they? Pincus and the team recruited from the local Shin Bet must surely have him and Lily under surveillance. And what about the possible leak in the Mossad? Ari drank more coffee, and then took a piece of buttered toast.

"Got any jam?" Ari smiled, clearly stalling.

"Jam, jelly, preserves. I've got it all." Scott never took his gaze off Ari's face. "You owe it to me Ari. I need to know what kind of threat you and Lily are under. You understand, as long as you are living under my roof, so to speak."

"Yeah, forget about the jam." Ari took a deep breath and began the lengthy tale of his recent travels from the Mount of Olives to the Sinai and back to the Greek Orthodox garden.

Scott sat perfectly still, listening as if he were at an academic lecture, until he heard the words, *Greek Orthodox Garden*. "You mean you were hiding right next to the City of David site?"

Ari hung his head sheepishly. "I spotted you the first day I arrived. Just a glimpse before I hid beneath a big fig tree that straddles the properties."

"Does Lily know all this?" Scott asked.

"Lily is aware I am compelled by forces I don't entirely understand. But if I am honest, I don't fully understand the nebulous relationship Lily has with the archangel Michael. What I do know is Lily walks in the light." Ari stroked his jaw then looked straight at Scott before continuing. "Not so for my brother Reza. Darkness overshadows everyone connected with the Mahdi Brotherhood."

Scott brusquely replied, "There's nothing that can't be fixed." He leaned forward placing a comforting hand on Ari's shoulder. "Oh, before I forget, somebody delivered a letter for you this morning. I meant to give it to you in the garden."

Ari jumped up throwing off his hand. "Who knows I'm here? An Israeli?"

"By his appearance and his accent, I would say Palestinian."

"Did he look like me, but older?"

"Nothing like you, I can say with certainty. Why don't you open the letter and find out?"

Ari sat down again at the table, smoothed the square envelope with his fingers, and then opened it with the butter knife. As he read the contents, his breathing discernibly slowed down in direct ratio to the rage that burned inside him.

"I can't face him again. Not after he tried to kill my wife and child. It was too good to last—this peaceful garden, the little cottage." Ari crumpled the letter, threw it on the table and made for the door.

"Where are you going?" Scott said, alarm in his voice. "Who is the note from?"

"I'm going to kill my brother," Ari replied in a cold, flat voice.

Scott hurried after him. "Wait. Think of Lily and Abigail."

Ari turned but did not slow his pace. "I'm doing this for them."

"You being dead or in prison will not help them. Think man."

Ari violently slammed the door and rushed out the front gate. Scott did not try to stop him, but instead picked up the crumpled note and read it. At least he knew where Ari was going.

Chapter 20

Dressed in his newly-tailored suit, Reza cautiously opened the door to receive his early morning visitor. Why an emissary from the holy city of Mecca would choose such an inhospitable hour, he could not say. But he knew he must receive him, no matter the hour. His guest wore a western-style suit, much like his own. He also kept his beard trimmed and neat. Reza assumed this messenger dressed as inconspicuously as possible, for the same reason he himself did. They both knew that East Jerusalem, and particularly the American Colony Hotel, swarmed with foreign agents, and it would not be prudent to look like an Iranian or Saudi emissary.

Reza made a slight bow out of respect for his visitor's rank in the Mahdi Brotherhood, and ushered him into the sitting area of his two-room suite. After murmuring his name, or at least the name on his current passport, the man sat stone-faced on the silk-covered sofa.

"Can I offer you tea?"

The visitor spoke sharply, "Please do not take this to be a social visit."

"Of course, of course," Reza said, sounding anxious. He never could abide the Saudi members of the Brotherhood. Thanks be to Allah, they were few in number. *But not in wealth and influence*, he reminded himself.

"A bottle of mineral water would be welcome." Then the guest added, "Unopened." A sly smile flickered across his face as he took out a silver case, removed a cigarette, lit a match, and inhaled heavily.

Reza busied himself at the non-alcoholic bar in the dining area. He took a bottle of sparkling water from the mini bar, placed it next to a glass tumbler on a tray. Sweat began to dampen the collar of his shirt, but his hands remained steady. After placing the refreshments on the marble coffee table, he boldly took a seat in the leather wing-backed chair opposite the sofa.

Minutes passed in silence as his guest crushed out his smoke, broke the seal on the water, and filled the glass half-full. He delicately sipped once or twice then patted his lips with a handkerchief. "Now," he said, rather sharply, "let's get down to business."

"I am at your service," Reza replied in a humble but well-practiced manner.

"It has come to our attention that the Holy One, your half-brother, is having second thoughts about his mission."

Reza's mouth nearly dropped open in astonishment before he gained control of his features and simulated a look of mild surprise. "The Mahdi having second thoughts? Who would dare suggest such a thing?" Reza retorted. His heart rate sped up as adrenalin flooded his system. The Saudi branch of the Brotherhood must be hatching a nefarious plot to replace him as the second in command. They would not directly attack Ari. Or would they?

The visitor glanced at his well-buffed fingernails before replying, "We know he is still consorting with that woman and her child. The so-called she-devil you reported had been eliminated."

"Yes, but it is only a temporary situation. Part of the Holy One's dissimulation is to confound the Jews." Reza now openly wiped the sweat from his brow with his handkerchief. *Where does he get his information, perhaps from the bookshop owner?*

"Temporary you say?" He laughed harshly. "She will be dead soon, along with her child." The visitor looked directly at Reza, speaking in a whisper, "And her spouse."

Reza's features paled as he placed his hand over his heart. "Surely you can't mean the Mahdi will die."

"My dear man, all things are possible. You will assassinate your brother before the week is out."

Reza jumped up, visibly agitated and raised his hands in the air. "By God, I will not murder my own flesh and blood." He sank down again in the chair with his head in his hands.

"The Mahdi can disappear and reappear at will. If this brother of yours is truly the Twelfth Imam, the Holy One, death cannot hold him. He will return and fulfill his destiny."

Reza stared at his visitor without saying a word. Then he walked over to the mini bar, poured himself a glass of mineral water, and drank it in one long gulp.

After that he went to the window and opened it to let in fresh air, as he never could abide stale smoke. With his nerves now under control, he spoke in a low, modulated voice. "I will kill him. If he is who we think he is, he will be reincarnated. If he is an imposter, then I have done the right thing. Either way, I can do no wrong."

"Right, my friend, you cannot fail in this task. Your hands are clean, either way."

"And how do you suggest I carry out this order?"

"By any means you find suitable. But let me remind you a gas explosion in the night cannot be relied upon." The visitor shot Reza a grim smile. "I suggest you do it by your own hand."

Reza blanched and felt his stomach lurch as he thought of the possibilities. Should he strangle Ari or slit his throat? His brother was younger and fitter. There could be a struggle. No, poison had to be the answer, and that would suffice for the woman and her child as well.

"Consider the act done. I will do my duty." Reza bowed in humility. The visitor stood to indicate the audience over. Reza walked him to the door and sent him on his way under a pale golden Jerusalem sky.

Chapter 21

When Ari arrived by foot at the American Colony, he did not immediately enter the hotel, choosing instead to circle around to the back of the large compound. By this time, the raging surge of murderous revenge had dissipated sufficiently so that he could think in a cold, methodical manner. Once he found the suite number indicated in the note, he saw with satisfaction the location appeared secluded and would meet his purposes. Ari contemplated, if only momentarily, simply knocking on his brother's door, stepping inside, and instead of the familiar kiss on both cheeks, putting Reza in a strangle hold and snapping his neck. Reza would not have time to show fear or regret.

While pausing in the shadow of an overgrown bougainvillea bush, Ari took stock of the situation. He might carry out the murder and escape without detection, but what then? What about Lily and Abigail? How could he protect them from the Mahdi Brotherhood? And where would they go? Would Pincus provide new identities and a safe haven in a neutral country? Not likely if he was on the run for murder, fratricide to be exact. To gain that kind of aid from the Mossad, he would have to once again accomplish some act that coincided with their mission. Like prevent a terrorist attack of monumental proportions.

Just then he heard footsteps on the tiled stepping-stones which led through the garden to Reza's sequestered suite. A bellhop, dressed in a red velvet jacket, carried a tray with a pot of freshly brewed tea, and a folded copy of the morning newspaper. He rang Reza's bell, placed the tray on the doormat, and returned the same way he came, not waiting for a tip. Ari approached and stood to one side of the entrance where he could not be seen.

When the door opened and Reza bent to pick up the tray, Ari gently tapped his brother on the shoulder. Startled, Reza dropped the tray spilling the tea and ruining the morning paper.

"Brother," Reza managed to croak, before recovering his wits and reaching out to embrace Ari. "I did not expect you at such an hour."

"Shall we go inside, before we are seen?" Ari glanced to both sides. *I could so easily have broken his neck just now.*

"I assure you, this is a very private suite," Reza assured him, as they went inside.

Judging by the cigarettes butts in the ashtray and two glasses on the coffee table, Reza had recently entertained a visitor.

"I will call room service and ask them to replace the pot of tea." Reza laughed nervously. "How clumsy of me."

Ari took a seat on the sofa, aware of Reza's discomfort at his sudden appearance. "You sent me a note to visit you, did you not?" He stared intently at his brother's white countenance. He definitely detected a wary cast in Reza's expression. "Forget the room service. I want to talk about something far more important than your morning tea."

"I did not expect you to honor me with your presence so soon," Reza replied, still standing, but now looking offended.

"Come sit," Ari said brusquely. "I have been thinking a great deal about our previous conversation. Gog and Magog. Earthquakes." *Yes, this is precisely what I need to know more about. I must carry out a preemptive mission that will impress the Mossad enough to give us undercover status again.* "What were you telling me about the Sea of Galilee drying up like the Dead Sea?"

Reza, relieved to talk about any subject but the one paramount on his mind, launched into a full monologue about the *end of days*. "The Koran has declared Allah Most High created every living thing from water. I am quoting al-Anbiyah 21:30, as you know." Reza watched Ari nod in assent, and then continued. "Water, therefore, enjoys the status of mother of all living things including human beings. The Koran has further declared Allah's *Arsh,* the command center from which He controls the entire creation, rests on water. Again, you know the source, Hud 11:7."

Again Ari bowed his head slightly in agreement. "Yes, yes, but get to Gog and Magog."

Reza took a deep breath and continued at his own pedantic pace. "The religious way of life is one which insists on respect for water and which prohibits waste or excessive consumption of water. Yet the profile of Gog and Magog," he smiled in Ari's direction, "emerging from the Ahadth of the Prophet Mohammed is that of a people who consume water so excessively and foolishly that even the Sea of Galilee would eventually become dry. Hence they are the authors of their own destruction."

Ari nervously wet his lips before he spoke. "Can you put that in more modern terms?"

"In the vernacular, as you will, it means that as Gog and Magog, our Russian neighbors and allies to the North, journey to the grand finale in Jerusalem, they will drink out of the Sea of Galilee. Their excessive consumption of water will be such that nature will not be able to replenish it, and the water level would decrease until the sea would dry up." Reza's black brows merged as he scowled at Ari. "They not only corrupt and destroy the water resources of this region, but they commit *Fasad*, which will corrupt and destroy the water resources of the world. They have no respect for water."

Ari, by now somewhat puzzled, persisted in his questioning. "How does that impact us now? Here in Israel? I see no sign of the former Soviet Union mounting such an ambitious expedition against Jerusalem."

"Precisely. Our neighbors to the north are in no position to implement such an endeavor at this point in time. That is where you come in."

"Me?" Ari replied, his composure shaken.

"Only the Holy One can bring about the massive earthquake to cause the collapse of the Golan Heights, and bury the Sea of Galilee in ash and rubble." Reza poured himself another glass of mineral water.

Ari, recovering himself, asked sharply, "Remind me how I am to carry out this mission."

Reza visibly flinched at the tone in Ari's voice. "In Damascus, we have hidden a small atomic bomb, which, detonated underground, will activate the simmering volcanoes on the Golan. The act will set off a massive earthquake that will bring about the destruction of the Sea of Galilee."

"I see." Ari rubbed his chin in amazement. "With no water, Israel will cease to exist. The former Soviet Union's role will be eliminated. They, being infidels, will enter into hellfire in any case. Am I right?"

Reza smiled sadly. "Yes. That is their destiny."

Ari's expression remained grim. He looked at his hands carefully inspecting the cuticles. Moments passed in uneasy silence as neither spoke.

Reza nervously broke the impasse by asking, "What motivated you to visit me this morning?"

Ari flexed his strong fingers gauging their ability to efficiently choke the life out of Reza. "I came here this morning to inform you I'm finished with this charade as a monk. I've left the Greek Orthodox garden, and I don't plan to return."

Reza cautiously replied, "As you desire, most Holy One. What will you do next?"

"I will go to Damascus and set the plan in motion. Tell me exactly where the bomb is hidden."

Reza permitted himself a small smile that did not, however, lighten his eyes. "I have not been given the precise location. But you, Holy One, do not need me to show you the way."

Knowing he had been out-maneuvered by an expert in this deadly game of chess, Ari nodded his head in acknowledgment of his own supernatural powers which gave him the ability to see into the future. "I indeed know where and how to proceed." With that, Ari turned and left Reza's hotel suite with a curt *salaam*.

Chapter 22

Reza left his hotel on foot heading toward the Damascus Gate. Street vendors piled their goods on their carts. Shopkeepers inside the walls of the Old City unrolled their metal protective doors. Feral cats looked for a sunny place to curl up and sleep away the day. Reza asked a green grocer where he could find a pharmacy or a chemist. The man scratched his beard, studied Reza's handsome new suit and then pointed down an alley which led deep into the *souk*.

Reza soon found the ancient-looking shop advertising everything from aspirin to antibiotics. "*Ahlan*, welcome, peace be upon you," the proprietor said, greeting his first customer of the day.

Reza replied with the appropriate courteous response as he automatically scanned the premises, and then proceeded to browse around the shop as if interested in toothpaste and vitamins. Only when he was completely assured there were no other customers in the shop, did he ask the man if he was in fact a chemist. When certain of this fact, he proceeded to ask the man if he could recommend a poison that worked quickly and efficiently.

"What kind of pest do you have in mind? Rats are one thing. Dogs and cats are another. Or maybe it is a two-legged creature you need to eliminate." He choked back a chuckle when he observed the severe expression on Reza's face. "I didn't mean to offend you. I, ah, why don't you tell me what it is you need, enough of this foolish jesting. My wife always says my frivolous ways will get me into trouble one day." His voice tapered off into an awkward silence.

"I need a compound that is swift and deadly." Reza glared at the pharmacist with an intensity that implied no explanations would be forthcoming.

Gulping back any objections he may have had, the man motioned for Reza to follow him to a back room. Surrounded with shelves holding hundreds of different powders, pills and clear liquids, the pharmacist donned a white lab coat, and pulled on plastic gloves while Reza stood silently observing.

Reaching under the work counter, the man retrieved a glass jar filled with a grayish green powder. "Oleander leaves, deadly when ingested. The leaves have been ground to a fine powder, and then distilled to a lethal concentration." He proceeded to extract a minute amount with a thin spatula, putting it into a small vial. "This should take care of any pest infestation."

Reza cleared his throat before asking, "Do I need to dissolve this powder in a liquid?"

"Whatever your vermin like best. You can mix it with food, or in, let's say, a saucer of milk."

Reza reached inside his jacket and pulled out a wad of shekel notes. "This should cover it." Reza then turned and let himself out the front door. Striding down the dark, narrow lane he almost knocked over a rude Israeli who wasn't paying attention. Reza wanted to heap curses on the man's hapless head, but he refrained, not wanting to call attention to himself so near to the chemist shop.

* * * *

Later that day, Ari met with Motti Pincus in his office behind the Russian Compound. He related in brief detail what he'd learned from his brother about the stockpile of explosives, possibly including a small A-bomb hidden in Damascus.

"Plan to blow up the Golan, you say?" Pincus spoke in a tone that implied he'd heard it all and nothing could perturb him.

"These *mehablim*, terrorists, think such an act will trigger the dormant volcanoes." Ari shook his head in disbelief. "Then the violent eruptions will cause a lava flow to bury the Sea of Galilee in a mass of smoldering magma, thereby destroying Israel's water supply." Ari chose to withhold what Reza had said about Gog and Magog.

"Haven't we already been down this path? Didn't Lily prevent the poisoning of the Jordan River with her mystical almond twig?" Pincus fiddled with his empty pipe. "It's not that I doubt your sincerity, Ari, but this sounds preposterous."

"I'm giving you important intelligence. I wish I had more details to make you believe this is a serious threat."

"It's never easy to send an undercover team into Syria. And I know you aren't volunteering." Pincus stared hard at Ari and only looked away when the phone suddenly rang.

"Yes, he's here, sitting across from me. Really, how curious." Pincus put the phone down and stared at Ari.

Ari saw a look of pity in the Mossad officer's eyes quickly replaced with a cool look of appraisal. "Who was that and how does it concern me?" Ari asked with growing trepidation.

"The call was from one of the men assigned to follow your brother. It seems shortly after you left Reza's suite at the American Colony, he made a little visit to a pharmacist in the Old City. With a bit of friendly persuasion, the chemist revealed what he sold to your brother." Pincus paused for dramatic effect.

"Well, get on with it. Can't a man buy a sleep aid or a pain pill without you getting involved?" Ari snorted in annoyance. He refused to tell Pincus about his murderous thoughts and plans concerning his brother, but it bothered him to know they monitored his every move.

"Reza *joon*, your dear Reza, evidently bought a vial of poison capable of killing a man in minutes." Pincus didn't have to wait for Ari's reaction.

Ari smashed his fist on the desk with such force the phone bounced off onto the floor. While Pincus bent to retrieve it, Ari tried to control his emotions but unable to mask the unabashed anger in his voice said, "I'll kill *him* first."

"Hold on, man. Nobody is talking about murder here. We don't know Reza plans to use this poison on you." Pincus spoke in his conciliatory tone. "My man said something about exterminating vermin."

Ari laughed bitterly. "You think a five-star hotel like the American Colony has a rat problem?" Without waiting for a reply Ari stormed out of the office.

Chapter 23

Lily sat under the grape arbor while Abigail played at her feet. The peaceful, domestic scene belied the turbulent emotions which assailed her mind. Intuitively, she felt Ari intended to do something that would not benefit either of them. Furthermore, she felt strongly this ill-advised course of action involved his brother. *Reza has been a black cloud hanging over my head since the day I first encountered him in the Old City.*

Abigail looked up and focused her soft, brown eyes on her mother's face. When Lily smiled at her, she returned to the twigs she tried to pick up with her chubby fingers. "When your Abba returns this morning, I will insist on an explanation for his abrupt departure." At that moment, she turned at the sound of the front gate opening. "Ari, we're over here under the arbor."

Ari rounded the corner, smiling at the sight of his wife and daughter. His smile quickly left as he noted Lily's frown.

"Sit." Lily motioned to an empty lawn chair. "I've been in a state since you left this morning."

"Darling Lily, I have so much I need to tell you. But it's not easy, and I don't know where to start." He reached out and took Lily's hand and caressed it.

"Start with where you went after breakfast." She removed her hand from his and adjusted the folds of her skirt. "You can't just keep disappearing on us." She bent and patted Abigail's curls.

"Lily, look at me," he commanded gently. When she raised her eyes, he continued in a low voice. "I intended to kill Reza this morning, with my bare hands, no gun, and no knife, with these." He held up his hands.

Glancing to ascertain that Abigail remained happily engaged with her leaves and twigs, Lily felt her heart pound wildly before she responded, "And?"

"I didn't do it."

"Why not?" Her voice revealed her relief.

"I was thinking of the repercussions for Abigail and you. I thought first I needed to make a deal with Pincus to protect us with new identities, again."

"Yes, again, but this time with a child. No, Ari. I can't do that." She smiled faintly. "No matter how much I wish Reza did not exist in our lives." This time Lily reached out and took Ari's hand in hers. "So, then what *did* you do?"

"After paying a visit to my brother, I went to Pincus' office. While I was there, he got a phone call. They have Reza under surveillance, just like they do us." He paused to gauge Lily's response. When she just shrugged, he continued, "Right after my visit to Reza, they followed him to a chemist shop in the Old City. He purchased poison."

"You want to kill him, but he plans to poison you first?" Lily's eyes widened. "It doesn't make sense. Doesn't he adore you? Thinks you're the great Mahdi?"

"Maybe he doubts my true identity. What if he knows I am an imposter?"

"Are you?"

"Lily, you know I'm not their so-called Muslim messiah. Dan and Eli helped me to see how I have been brainwashed. I want nothing more to do with the Mahdi Brotherhood, but it's not as simple as just walking away."

"We can leave Israel, with or without the Mossad's help. We can start over in Australia, for instance," Lily blurted.

Ari turned a sad glance in Abigail's direction. "No, we have to stay and see this through. It's bigger than just the survival of our little family." Before he could continue, he was interrupted by the arrival of Professor Scott.

"Ah, here you are. Well, well, well." Scott appeared at a loss for more words. After an awkward silence hung in the air, he continued, "Now that you have returned from your morning errands, if you have time, I would like to make a little proposition to you."

Lily picked up Abigail and suggested they all go inside. "Tell us what you have in mind over a cup of tea or coffee."

Once inside the kitchen of the big house, Scott began to outline a scheme for Ari to become his assistant on the dig. "I know you're not trained in this discipline, but I can teach you the rudiments of how to take soil samples. I will, of course do all the lab work, but I can use a second pair of hands in the underground tunnels. What do you say?"

Lily nudged Ari in the ribs with her elbow urging him to respond. When he hesitated, she raised her hands in mock surrender. "I give up. What can I say?"

Scott looked from one to the other. "In lieu of the fact that you're not engaged in any regular employment that I can see, I thought you would jump at the chance. Especially since this work is done underground, completely out of sight of the public."

Lily took this moment to light a fire under the teakettle and pull some cups off the shelf. She bustled about making hot drinks with Abigail hitched on one hip.

Meanwhile, Scott laid out his proposition to Ari. "You know of course, the history of the Gihon Spring. It's situated outside the city walls in the Kidron Valley. Since it was the only year-round water supply, the early inhabitants of Jerusalem built a subterranean water system to channel the spring water into the walled city.

Eventually, Hezekiah had tunnels built so the people could draw water without being exposed to the enemy."

Ari nodded his head, acknowledging his familiarity with this bit of history. Lily placed steaming cups of coffee in front of both of them. Then Scott continued, "You've probably walked through either the wet tunnel or the dry channel."

"Yes, a few years ago. I remember the water coming up to my hip. Not unpleasant in the summer time, but I wouldn't recommend it during the rainy season. The tunnel is about 500 meters long, right?"

"Yes, that's about right; however, my work at the moment is drilling for pollen samples in the dry channel. I need an assistant to hand me the equipment and at the same time hold the flashlight."

Ari said nothing as he stirred two teaspoons of sugar into his black coffee.

Lily sat down at the table with Abigail in her lap. She turned to Scott with a pale face and trembling lips. "Do you work anywhere near Absalom's Tomb?"

"No," Scott answered. "I never cross the Kidron. I enter the City of David at the visitors' entrance at the top, or I drive down the lane and park at the bottom of the *wadi* near the Siloam pool."

"Why does it matter?" Ari asked. "I can see Lily's upset about something." He stared hard at Scott.

"While you were away, I gave Lily a walking tour outside the city walls. When we attempted to cross the Kidron stream bed, she saw something that frightened her." Scott looked at Lily to see if she wanted him to continue.

Lily put one hand over her eyes before responding in a low voice. "I saw the shadow of Lucifer lurking behind Absalom's Tomb. Don't ask how I knew who it was, I just did. Also, I could smell something awful coming from the creek bed. Even though it was dry, I had the feeling I would drown if I attempted to cross it." She shuddered at the memory and hugged her daughter tight.

Ari put his arm around her. "You never told me this."

"Well, so much has happened in the meantime, how could I?" Lily forced a smile. "Anyway, Scott saw nothing. He thought it was just my overwrought nerves." Then she laughed out loud. "I told this to the agent that follows me everywhere. He carefully wrote the name Lucifer in his little notebook."

Both Ari and Scott laughed ruefully with her. She added, "They already think I'm *meshugana.*"

"Pincus certainly doesn't think you're crazy, but he doesn't know how to categorize you or me. We continue to confound all his expectations," Ari said.

"Yes, well, mine also. I have never encountered the likes of you two," Scott responded. "But what is your answer? Will you work for me?"

Lily and Ari exchanged knowing glances, each looking to the other for affirmation. Lily responded first with a slight nod of her head. Ari took that as a positive and reached out to shake Scott's hand. "Partners it is. When do we start?"

"Tomorrow morning at daybreak. I have access to the site at all times, and the night watchman will let us in before the residents of Silwan are up and about. I assume you want to stay out of sight as much as possible." Not waiting for a response, Scott stood up and left the kitchen saying something about a mountain of paperwork to be tackled in his office.

Chapter 24

The morning star glowed faintly in the predawn darkness as Professor Scott loaded his equipment into the tiny Fiat. Before he opened the gate, Ari had already concealed himself under a blanket in the backseat. Any watchers on the street, Shin Bet or Reza's people, would only see the professor doing what he did nearly every morning. Driving slowly through the narrow lanes of East Jerusalem, Scott approached the Old City walls from the north, with the Mount of Olives on his left. The Garden of Gethsemane lay shrouded in darkness, as were the nearby churches; even though Scott knew the nuns and brothers would have long since been about their morning prayers. Approaching Dung Gate he turned left into the visitors' parking lot. His Fiat had a decal that allowed him to park for a monthly fee, rather than the steep daily rate imposed on tourists.

Judging by the two other vehicles in the lot, he was not the first to begin the day's work at the City of David. Nevertheless, he looked carefully about before he whispered to Ari that it looked safe.

Together they crossed the lane and entered the plaza at the visitors' entrance. The security man acknowledged Scott's greeting and the introduction of his new assistant. Ari nodded his head but didn't give his name. The security man shrugged and wrote something in his notebook. They quickly crossed the metal platform overlooking the Gihon Spring fortifications and then climbed down a spiral staircase deep into the bowels of the earth. Weak electric bulbs lighted their way. The air smelled dank and musty but not unpleasant. It felt cool and Scott was glad he wore a long-sleeved shirt. He glanced approvingly over at Ari who wore a baseball hat pulled low on his head almost covering his eyes.

Scott paused to point out a Muslim prayer niche dating from the Ottoman period. Then they passed the Gihon spring where it welled up in a cave, visible through an iron grille.

They spent the next few hours coring in the dry channel. Around nine a.m. Scott suggested they stop for a break. Leading the way, he led Ari through a labyrinth of tunnels and large and small chambers under various stages of excavation, until they finally emerged at the lower end of the site near the half-exposed pool of Siloam. The morning sun, already hot, felt good as they sat on the ancient steps and drank their black coffee and ate bread and cheese.

Scott noticed Ari staring at the overgrown fig tree separating the dig site from the garden belonging to the Greek Church where he had only recently hidden. He understood why Ari pulled his cap down further on his forehead.

Ari put down his sandwich, evidently no longer hungry.

"That place still haunts you?" Scott stared at the trees on the other side of the barbed wire.

"I mourned the death of my wife and child there. I didn't want to go on living." Ari threw his half-eaten sandwich to a feral cat scrounging under the fig tree. "Reza tried to kill them in a gas explosion, and now he wants to poison me."

"I guess you'd better watch what you eat and drink." Scott finished his sandwich and wiped his hands on his trousers. "I buy all my groceries from an Arab market on Saladin Street. Do you think it's safe?"

"Maybe from now on, it would be prudent to buy your food in Mahane Yehuda, where you or I are not known."

"You mean the open-air market off Jaffa Road? Not far from the bus station?" Scott asked.

"Yes, the Jewish market." Ari abruptly stood. "I need to warn Lily not to eat or drink anything outside the house. No doubt they still want her and Abigail dead." His mouth turned down in an angry scowl.

"Here, use my cell phone to call her."

Ari let the phone ring for several long moments with no answer. "I have to go back."

"She could be in the garden or in the cottage and can't hear the phone ringing." Scott tried to placate Ari, but knew it was in vain. "Leave by the bottom gate. It's quicker than winding back through the tunnels. Take the path around the Old City. On foot, you will get there quicker than trying to drive at this time of day."

* * * *

Ari wanted to run but knew it would attract unwanted attention, so he walked as briskly as he thought feasible. He darted between the stream of cars and tour buses heading for the Western Wall. Skirting the walls, he strode past the East Jerusalem post office, up Saladin Street and down an alley. Standing outside the gate of the House of Peace, he paused to get his breath and let himself in with a key. "Lily," he shouted as he took the front steps two at a time. He raced through the empty house and out the back through the kitchen. "Lily," he shouted again inside the cottage. Getting no answer, he dashed out to the grape arbor where Abigail liked to play under the shady leaves. Berating himself for not warning them to stay inside the compound, he threw himself down into a lawn chair, raking his hands through his already disheveled hair. Suddenly he jumped up and ran for Scott's office. Dialing Pincus's private number he felt his heart pounding in his ears.

Without identifying himself, knowing Pincus would have caller ID, he tried to control his voice as he asked, "Who is monitoring Lily?"

"I believe Benny is, why?" Pincus asked in a calm voice.

"They've left the house in East Jerusalem. I've got to warn Lily not to eat or drink anything in public."

"I understand," Pincus immediately replied. "I'll get word to Benny now." With that he hung up.

* * * *

At that moment, Lily strolled along King George Street with Abigail tucked into a baby carrier on her back. She slowed down at a kiosk and bought a borekes and a bottle of orange juice. Lifting the still warm pastry to her mouth, she started to take a bite when a hand reached out and sent the borekes flying. Startled, she turned to see Benny smiling at her. "You, you..." At a loss for words, she slapped him smartly across the cheek.

"Hey, calm down. I'm only following orders."

Lily's eyes narrowed as she glared at him and demanded, "Whose orders?"

"Apparently your husband contacted the boss and said it was imperative you neither eat nor drink anything outside the house." He reached out and took the bottle of orange juice away from a stunned Lily.

A small crowd of onlookers had by now gathered around them. One gray-haired woman told Lily not to take any more abuse. She volunteered to call the police. A young man offered his assistance. The kiosk seller wrung his hands in distress but remained safely behind his stall.

Benny flashed a badge with one hand, so quickly no one could read it, but it had the hoped-for effect. The crowd melted away, some muttering, others just shrugging their shoulders.

By this time, Abigail, upset by the loud voices and the stress she heard in her mother's voice, began to wail piteously. Lily slipped the shoulder harness off and held her daughter close to her bosom. "Darling, it's only that mean old Benny again."

Benny frowned, obviously not happy to be thought of as the bad guy again. He took Lily's arm and steered her down the street toward Jaffa Road. "Do you want to speak to your husband?" He handed her his cell phone.

Lily snatched it out of his hand without comment then realized she didn't know what number to dial.

"Punch in 038. That's a direct line to Pincus's office. I believe your husband can be reached there."

Lily did as instructed. In a few seconds she spoke to Ari, who quickly reassured her everything was *col besedar*. "Just don't eat or drink in public. You know why."

Lily sadly affirmed she did know why. "When will you be home?"

"Soon, I'm on my way now."

"Me too," Lily replied and hung up, not wanting to say anymore in front of Benny.

Chapter 25

Reza sat and stared at the package, wrapped in plain, brown paper, and tied with a bit of twine. In all his years as an emissary of the Mahdi Brotherhood, he had never found himself in this position. There had been difficult years when his very life had been threatened by the forces which wanted to stifle the Mahdi Brotherhood. But, he had survived again and again. He acknowledged the hidden identity of the Holy One was complicated by the very fact that Ari had been born of the stock of Jacob, and at the same time, was a direct descendent of the prophet Mohammed, blessed be his name. Reza's mouth turned into a grimace as he thought of all of Ari's Jewish connections that had been eliminated. There remained only the woman called Lily and her child.

Fingering the package, Reza slowly undid the twine and removed the paper wrapping. The small vial of deadly poison looked so innocuous sitting there on his coffee table next to the bowl of oranges. The minutes and hours passed by as if in a dream as Reza contemplated first one scheme and then another as he formulated his plans to eliminate Lily and her baby. With those two dead and buried, he must find some way to spare his brother the agony of actually dying a painful death by a lethal dose of the poison sitting right here on the table. Reza then contemplated the possibility Ari was not capable of resurrection. No, that thought was unacceptable to him. The Mahdi could appear and disappear at will with complete mastery over life and death. Not like the imposter, Issa, whose followers claimed had risen from the dead, but who had in fact been taken down from the cross and went on to live a long life.

Reza got up from the sofa and turned on the floor lamp, dispelling the shadows that had gathered in the corners of the room. It was nearly dusk and time for prayer. With a sigh of resignation, he performed his ablutions, and then knelt on his prayer rug facing Mecca. When he finished praying, he called room service and ordered a plate of plain rice, lamb, and yoghurt.

While eating his dinner, the answer to his present dilemma came to him. It would be too difficult to get close enough to Lily and her child to actually poison them. He would employ a different plan. It would have to look like an ordinary accident. He smiled as he wiped a bit of food off his lips. It would not be so difficult to monitor their movements, their goings and comings from the big house. Why not have Lily run over by an out-of-control vehicle? Ari would be spared, and he would have no choice but to embrace his destiny as the Holy One. There would be no reason why Ari would not then use the atomic weapons hidden in Damascus. That act would surely satisfy those in the Brotherhood who doubted Ari's credentials.

The next morning, as Reza walked about the East Jerusalem neighborhood, he noted the number of construction projects in progress, a new hotel going up on one corner, road work blocking traffic on another. Vehicles were constantly backed up as dump trucks and heavy earth movers and bulldozers crowded the narrow streets. Even as Reza narrowly avoided being run over by a Caterpillar by jumping back on the sidewalk at the last moment, it came to him how the assassination of Lily could be carried out.

An out-of-control bulldozer did not stretch the imagination. Lily and her daughter would be crushed to death in an instant. It would not be difficult to recruit an East Jerusalem Arab to carry out the deed. With promises of a glorified martyrdom for not only himself but his entire extended family, any number of out-of-work Palestinians could be recruited. And of course, it would look better if a crowd of pedestrians were targeted, not just Lily, the more Jews who died the better. Of course, the bulldozer driver would be shot dead by an armed passerby. With no witness to betray the Mahdi Brotherhood's part in the mayhem, Reza would see to it that the dead Palestinian's family would be more than adequately provided for in both material goods and emotional support.

Feeling elated by imagining such possibilities, Reza decided to pay a visit to the Noble Sanctuary where he would humbly pray and give thanks to Allah for his providential enlightenment. He quickly walked through Damascus Gate and continued straight through the *souk*, and then turned at the narrow lane that ended at the entrance to the Temple Mount. Israeli Border Patrol soldiers along with Palestinian police officers stopped everyone who desired to enter the esplanade. Jews and Christians were politely turned away. Young Muslim men, who might want to create a riot, were also turned away.

Reza's gray beard gained him entrance, but the guards advised the mosque was temporarily closed for repairs. Reza nodded in acknowledgement and proceeded to the area north of the Al-Aqsa Mosque where he knew he would find the structure called the Dome of the Rock. He had wanted to visit this in the first place, not the usually crowded mosque. He headed to the revered Foundation Stone where according to tradition, Abraham had bound his son for sacrifice, and from which Mohammed had ascended to heaven after his miraculous nocturnal journey.

Standing by the octagonal structure, he bowed his head in acknowledgment of the monument's special aura. Here he vowed to complete his mission. Time seemed to stand still, the very air suspended in a stillness that echoed the ancient stone's silent witness. After some moments, Reza raised his eyes to gaze at the swallows swooping across the plaza in graceful arcs.

* * * *

Later that evening, back in his hotel suite, Reza arranged for the bookshop owner to meet with him. They agreed he would recruit two men, one as a backup in case the first failed. Both men would have to know how to operate heavy equipment, such as a bulldozer. Also, a third man would be recruited to monitor Lily's comings and goings. A pattern would eventually be identified, and the details set in motion for the deadly accident.

Reza made it clear the men did not have to be members of the Mahdi Brotherhood. It was better for all concerned if Palestinians did the job, young men eager to be martyred for their cause.

Reza could see this last objective did not sit well with the bookstore owner. "Do I see doubt in your eyes?"

The man looked away from Reza's penetrating gaze, obviously uncomfortable. "It's not my place to object."

"But you have objections, do you not?"

"Do there need to be more martyrs for the cause? Our young men die as if they were no more than fruit falling prematurely from the tree."

Reza sighed deeply. He did not like the idea of more dead Palestinians. Far too many youth had died needlessly, in his point of view. Maybe he should rethink the option of poison. That plan would not necessitate someone sacrificing his life. "Hold everything I have told you close to your heart. We may be able to accomplish our goal another way. You are right, let us try to preserve the lives of our fine young men." Reza knew this way of thinking did not fit in with the overall philosophy of the Mahdi

Brotherhood, sacrifice and martyrdom being the highest form of worship. But more and more, Reza had found his thoughts deviating from the established line. This he kept strictly to himself. Not that he had any objection to getting rid of Lily. She had no place in the end-time scenario. He would have to reconsider how to administer the poison.

"Go home, my good man. Forget I summoned you tonight. Forget everything I asked you to do on behalf of the Brotherhood. Tell no one of this visit."

Reza closed the door on his bewildered, but obviously relieved visitor. He went to his bedroom and picked up the vial of poison, balancing it in his hand. What had transpired when he visited the Dome of the Rock yesterday? What should he do?

Chapter 26

Lily felt she had been sidelined by Scott and Ari as they set off every morning to work in the City of David. Of course, she had Abigail to attend to, but the little girl was easy to entertain and feed between naps. These duties did not occupy the many hours of the day, and motherhood, no matter how satisfying, did not erase the sense of dread which hovered over her whenever she thought of Reza and the detested Mahdi Brotherhood. Intuitively, she felt the nasty business at Absalom's tomb was connected to Reza.

"We're going out, *motek*," Lily said one afternoon. "Let's take a ride in your new stroller."

She unfolded the lightweight, portable carriage Ari had bought recently in the *shuk*. "We'll go visit Uncle Eli and Dan."

With Abigail happily seated in the stroller, they passed by the Garden Tomb, which already had a steady stream of pilgrims pouring in the gates. At the main avenue, she pushed harder as the road wound uphill to Jaffa Road. Opposite the Notre Dame Hotel, she waited for a green light and proceeded across the busy intersection. From there it was just a quick downhill walk to Jaffa Gate. The view of the Old City walls never failed to thrill her no matter how many times she passed this way. Her heart always beat a little faster as she approached what they called the Citadel of David.

She felt fortunate to find Eli and Dan at home, and they were willing to watch Abigail for an hour while Lily performed what she called an important errand.

Quickly, before they could change their minds, Lily walked as fast as her long legs would carry her around the city walls until she came to the promontory overlooking Absalom's Tomb. She remained determined to conquer her fear and face the devil that lurked there in the shadows. She stood at the observation point, designed as a small theater, with paving stones in the center depicting the plan of the Kidron Valley tombs. To the east, she could see the Mount of Olives, covered with the small tombstones of the Jewish cemetery. At the foot of the slope, she gazed at the monumental tombs of the Second Temple period. Her eyes searched for, and easily found the conical pyramid that topped the cube-shaped monument hewn out of limestone.

The identification of Absalom's Tomb was, of course, erroneous. Lily knew from her history lessons in Hebrew School that the monument had been built more than a thousand years after the time of Absalom. However, teachers and parents never tired of telling of the custom of how people threw a stone at the monument to call down a curse on the rebellious son, Absalom, who had tried to usurp the throne of his father, King David.

Lily took a deep breath, and subconsciously looked heavenward as if for advice or comfort, as she set off down the path. She crossed the dry Kidron stream with no difficulty and encountered no obnoxious stench. She allowed herself to smile, grateful she did not have Abigail with her and so far, there appeared nothing amiss.

Reaching the base of the monument, she gazed at the Doric frieze on the top of the cube, along with an Egyptian cornice. With a flourish, she pulled out of her back pocket, a thin paper pamphlet she'd picked up in Scott's office. It described in detail the opening in the monument which led to a small burial chamber. It was too high up, and way too small for Lily to even contemplate trying to enter. In any case, centuries ago, tomb robbers had stolen anything of interest. No, she hoped to find something more ephemeral. Why had the vision of Lucifer confronted her here, and why had it appeared only to her and not to Scott?

Quickly scanning the pamphlet, the kind every tourist picked up and never bothered to read, she noted that Absalom's Tomb served as the *nefesh*, or soul, a monument or stone marking the grave and commemorating the persons buried there. Reading more, she learned the object of real value lay behind the monument, the Cave of Jehoshaphat—an imposing burial cave with a doorway cut into the rock behind the tomb.

"I never knew it was there," Lily said, quietly. "Maybe, what I'm looking for is hidden from the public's eyes. Jewish tourists like to throw a stone and say, 'take that, you rebellious son', but the thing of value might be the cave."

Lily hesitated for only a moment and looked over her shoulder toward Silwan where Ari and Scott worked together underground. Maybe it would be better to wait for them to go with her. After all, she had not anticipated going into any caves and had not brought a flashlight or ropes. The sun rose high overhead, and she decided to just peek in at the rock opening of the Cave of Jehoshaphat. She duly noted the gable over the entrance decorated with carved floral designs. Standing in the entrance, the light remained good enough to count several burial chambers branching off from the entrance. But she did not go in any farther to investigate. She would come back with Ari and adequate equipment.

She did not get the sense of an evil presence as she had with Scott, but her highly-strained nerves hummed with a surge of adrenalin. She fought the urge to turn and run. Shading her eyes, she found evidence of recent visitors, judging by the many footprints in the dusty entrance. Focusing on the dirt and gravel, she saw what could be scrape marks, which indicated a large object had been pushed or shoved into the cave. Somebody had hidden something here.

Retracing her steps, she returned as quickly as possible to Dan and Eli's apartment in the Armenian Quarter. Her cheeks were flushed, but she tried to hide her excitement from the brothers' curious gaze. She gathered up her little darling, who did not appear to have missed her in the least. Thanking her friends for giving her what she called an "hour's respite" from the task of mothering, she bade them goodbye and hurried back to the cottage behind Scott's house.

That night when Ari returned home, tired and covered in dust, she waited until he'd showered and eaten before telling him of her adventure.

"Jehoshaphat's Cave?" Ari bellowed so loud Scott could have heard him in the main house. "Why would you go there? I thought the Kidron Valley freaked you out?"

"You know how I get these feelings. I just had to go there and put my mind at ease. This time I found no sign of Lucifer lurking about."

"As if he ever was," Ari mumbled.

"Well," Lily responded, trying hard not take umbrage, "you'll be relieved to know I didn't enter the cave. It branches off into what the brochure said is eight chambers. I thought it best to wait and return with you."

"Did you?" Ari said as he reached out and put his arms around his wife. "It's all too dangerous, poison, or exploding gas heaters, or a fall down a deep chasm." His features tightened. "You didn't take Abigail did you?"

"Of course not." Lily wriggled out of Ari's arms. "I dropped her off at the brothers' apartment for an hour. They were delighted to watch her."

Ari shook his head while Lily cleared the table of their simple meal. "What possessed you to go there? What did you hope to find?"

Lily spoke with her back to him as she washed the supper plates in the small sink. "It has something to do with Reza. I just don't know what." When finished, she dried her hands on her skirt and sat down again at the table. "When you have a free day, let's go there together and check it out. It may be nothing, just my imagination." Whether by intent or accident, she forgot to mention the footprints at the entrance to the cave.

Ari, visibly agitated, grunted something unintelligible in reply.

"I take that as a yes, you'll go with me. I can't ask the brothers to look after Abigail again. They were sweet about it, but I could see the relief in their eyes when I picked her up." Lily stared into space as she thought about finding a suitable babysitter. "I don't suppose we could ask Benny, my Mossad minder."

"Don't even think about it." Ari laughed. "Can you picture him entertaining our daughter? But speaking of Benny, how do you know he didn't follow you to the Kidron Valley today?"

"Well, I didn't see him, now that you mention it. He could have been lurking behind some boulder." Lily frowned, not relishing the possibility she'd been followed. "What about asking Scott? He takes a day off now and then, and he wouldn't have to do much, just feed Abby lunch and put her down for a nap."

Ari shrugged, lifting a shoulder in silent acknowledgement that Lily would get her way. "I'll leave it to you. Ask him, and if he agrees, I'll go with you. A quick look around, in and out. No rappelling down black holes, no crawling through narrow passages that lead God knows where. You say there are eight burial chambers leading off the entrance? We'll check them out to put your mind at ease. And I don't think this has anything to do with my brother."

Lily patted his cheek. "Thanks for being so understanding." She felt he would not oppose her plan yet icy fingers ran up her spine causing her to feel chilled to the bone. She quietly got up and shut the windows in the cottage, then put on a sweater.

Chapter 27

Overnight the temperature changed as hot, dry air blew in from Saudi Arabia, covering Jerusalem in a thin blanket of dust. *I hate a khamsin, good we're leaving Abigail inside with Scott.* Lily noticed the professor had already closed the metal shutters on all the windows of the big house. She did the same in the cottage. They had asked Scott to look after their daughter, and after only a small pause, he had acquiesced. Lily knew, of course, he'd been a bit nervous about babysitting, never having been a father.

They planned to leave shortly after breakfast, after stockpiling Scott's kitchen with enough baby food, diapers, and toys to last a week.

"How long did you say you'd be away?" Scott asked looking at the pile on the kitchen table.

Ari laughed low in his throat. "Not more than a few hours."

Lily added, "It's good to be prepared."

"Where did you say you're going?"

Ari stared at Lily as if to say, you tell him.

Lily scowled back as she lifted a shoulder in a delicate gesture of surrender. "We didn't say." Then she rearranged a few items on the kitchen table, apparently looking for something. "Ah, here's the spare pacifier." She looked directly at Scott. "Abby's teething and sometimes fusses. This helps."

"Duly noted," Scott replied in a determined voice before asking, "And the answer to my question?"

"Just tell him," Ari said. "Someone needs to know. In case anything happens to us."

Lily replied, "Okay, we're going to Absalom's Tomb." She looked up to see Scott's reaction. His face showed no surprise or any emotion. "I've conquered my fear of the place, and I feel compelled to investigate the caves behind the tomb. You know, the Cave of Jehoshaphat. There's a rock opening cut there. It looks accessible."

Ari now jumped into the conversation. "I couldn't talk her out of it, so the safest thing is to go along and see what there is to see." He quickly added, "I've got a rope and flashlights. We're checking out the eight burial chambers off the main entrance. No spelunking, in case you envision us diving down black holes."

Scott shook his head and then put out his arms to take Abigail. "She'll be content here in my kitchen, I dare say, for a few hours. You'd best get on with it."

Staying off the main streets, Ari and Lily went on foot through the back alleys of East Jerusalem, coming out near the top of Wadi Joz, and then slipping unseen, into the Kidron Valley from the slopes of the Mount of Olives. Lily tucked her auburn curls inside a baseball cap like her husband's. They both wore dusty blue jeans and faded work shirts, making them look like two ordinary day laborers. Ari carried the equipment in a small backpack. Each had a canteen of water, necessary during a *khamsin*. They passed no one as they approached the entrance to the cave.

"Feeling okay?" Ari turned to Lily following close behind him. "Are you picking up any sense of danger, anything spooky?"

Lily grimaced. "Are you mocking me?"

"No, sweetheart, I mean it. I know you have a gift for the supernatural."

Lily relaxed her shoulders, closed her eyes, and breathed in through her nose as if sniffing something in the air. Sensing nothing unusual, she nodded for Ari to proceed.

"Right," Ari responded with little enthusiasm. "Wait at the entrance while I make a quick check of the first cave. Follow when I give the signal."

* * * *

Ari cautiously stepped inside. He aimed his flashlight over the floor and saw scuff marks in the dust. He raised the beam to the ceiling, and moved it slowly around the entire cave. Seeing nothing to arouse his suspicions, he whistled for Lily to join him. When she stood just inside the entrance, he asked, "How do you know there're exactly eight burial chambers leading off this main entrance? I can make out two, maybe three other openings branching off."

"Remember, I told you I bought a guide book and looked at the drawings and diagrams of the cave. You know I would never explore this creepy place unprepared."

"Creepy?"

"You know what I mean." She paused and slowly turned her head from side to side as if listening for someone or something. "It's here." Her voice quavered.

"What's here?"

"That evil spirit, it's back." She stood close enough to Ari for him to feel her breath on his cheek. "Something is definitely wrong here. Let's go home."

Ari took her cold hand in his. "You can wait outside if you want."

After a long pause she replied weakly, "No, let's get it over with."

They entered the first opening on the left which led to four more caves carved into the hillside. They were empty, apparently looted by the grave robbers of earlier centuries. The acrid smell of bat dung weighed heavily in the air.

"There should be more caves on the other side of the main one," Lily whispered in Ari's ear. "I don't know what I expect to find here, but it has something to do with your brother, Reza."

Ari stiffened, dropping Lily's hand. "What's he got to do with these caves?" Ari's voice held undisguised anger.

"I don't know. Let's forget I said anything."

Ari grunted in agreement. "We'll check out the other four caves as quickly as possible and get out of here."

In cave number seven, as Ari ran his flashlight beam over the floor, just as he had in the previous six, he motioned for Lily to stop. "Look here. Do you see the disturbance in the dust?"

"Yes," Lily responded, "Looks like something heavy was dragged across the floor." They followed the tracks until they disappeared at the far wall.

Ari bent down on one knee to examine where the scuff marks ended then he froze and motioned for Lily to get down. "I hear voices in the outer cave," he whispered in her ear. Quickly scanning the rough-hewn walls he noticed a shallow crevice on the opposite side. Pulling Lily behind him, he hid them both out-of-sight and turned off his light.

Moments later, they heard two men arguing in Arabic. Ari's knowledge of Arabic was limited, but he could tell by their accent they were not Palestinians. Maybe, as he later told Lily, Saudi or Jordanian. The two men, dressed like construction workers in heavy boots and hard hats, entered the cave shining their lights on the wall where the track marks ended. The taller one, evidently in charge, pressed his open palms on the rough wall. A slender opening appeared, revealing a small chamber.

From his crouched position in the crevice, Ari could not see what the hidden chamber held. But he could hear the tall man grunt as he lifted something heavy. Then the two men exchanged more sharp words in Arabic. It sounded to Ari as if the taller man rebuked the other one, whose voice appeared to be pleading. Although it felt like an eternity to Ari and Lily, the two men left the hidden chamber after only a few minutes, still arguing as the wall closed up behind them.

Ari placed his hand on Lily's mouth, signaling her not to say a word. They waited another five minutes, with their muscles cramping in their bent legs, before they crept out of their hiding place.

Maintaining silence both switched on their flashlights and inspected the opposite wall. Ari approached first with outstretched hands. He ran his fingers over the rough stone with palms open like he had observed the other man do. As expected, an opening appeared as he triggered some hidden device. Lily followed close on his heels as he cast his light. A heavy container sat on the floor within. Although shaped like a coffin, or an ancient stone sarcophagus, it definitely appeared of modern construction.

Lily moved her beam of light over the metal box trying to decipher the lettering on the lid. "Can you make this out?" she whispered.

"It's the Arabic alphabet, but it seems to be Persian writing," Ari replied, now more puzzled than ever.

Lily stifled a cry and took a step backward. "Didn't I say Reza is connected to this place?"

Ari ignored Lily's implied rebuke and continued to study the markings on the container. "I don't know what's written here, but I recognize the universal symbols for material that is highly dangerous or toxic."

"I say we leave now," Lily responded. "I have a very bad feeling."

"I thought I might try to lift the lid. I heard that guy grunting like he lifted something heavy. It'll only take a minute."

"No! Don't open it," Lily spoke between clenched teeth.

Alarmed, Ari turned and faced her. "Hey, you've seen too many movies. This isn't the ark of the covenant." But he did step away from the container.

"My intuition tells me to run out of here, now." Lily grabbed Ari's arm and pulled him towards the opening in the wall.

Before Ari could react, they heard footsteps in the next chamber. Ari immediately pushed Lily behind him as he slipped a hunting knife from his sock. The silence in the cave grew electrifying, causing the hair on the back of his neck to stand up. Folding himself into a half crouch he growled at Lily to take cover behind the metal container.

She did as she was told but remained standing. "They'll have to kill us both," she whispered back to Ari.

"No one is killing anyone." The shadow at the doorway stepped into the chamber. "You can drop your knife, Ari."

"Benny?"

"Yes. I got worried when I saw the two Arabs enter and then leave the cave. I don't know what I expected to find. Well, rather, I expected to find the two of you with your throats slit."

Trembling with nervous tension, Ari stood up, sheaved his knife back in the holder in his sock, and reached out to take Lily's arm. "It took you long enough to get to us, if that's what you thought."

"I phoned Pincus for backup as they entered the cave. He'll be here any minute."

"For once, I'm glad to see you," Lily said. She appeared to fight back tears. "I was suggesting to Ari we get out of here when you showed up."

Benny grunted something under his breath and took a few steps to take a closer look at the metal box. "What do we have here, obviously not antiquities."

Ari laughed bitterly. "Look at those symbols."

Benny methodically ran his flashlight over the lid. "From what I can decipher, those indicate we have a nuclear weapon here." He laughed a tight, mirthless laugh. "Nothing connected with you guys surprises me."

Ari's head jerked up. "This doesn't belong to us."

"I follow you here. Two Arabs then join you. What am I supposed to think?"

Lily burst out in a torrent of words, trying to explain why they were there and how wrong he was, and how Benny's boss would understand.

Benny snorted as he held back scornful laughter. "We'll see what Motti Pincus has to say. He should be here any minute."

They walked to the cave entrance.

As they emerged, Pincus arrived with two plainclothes officers. Army snipers crouched on the walls of the Old City opposite the cave. An ambulance, with its siren off, waited near the entrance to the City of David, and a helicopter hovered above the Mount of Olives, causing tourists to look up in puzzlement as if at the Second Coming.

With a grim nod, he acknowledged Ari and Lily, alive and well. "You better have a good explanation," Pincus spat tersely in Benny's direction. "I expected to find a blood bath, not to mention a god-awful standoff."

"Come see." Benny pointed at the entrance to the cave.

"Is it secure?" Pincus asked automatically.

"Depends on how you define secure." He paused dramatically as he stared ahead. "We might need a bomb disposal squad."

"Let me be the judge of that." Pincus strode into the rough opening with Benny and Ari close behind. All three emerged back into the sunlight within two minutes. Pincus's face looked like a gray mask as he made a call on his cell phone for an army specialist in disarming nuclear weapons.

"I want to talk to you two," he barked at Ari and Lily. "We can't be seen leaving the area together, so I suggest you start walking towards the Rockefeller. I'll meet you in the courtyard."

"What if the museum is closed?" Ari then added, "It usually is this time of the year."

"Just go. I'll see to it that they are expecting you at the guard station."

Chapter 28

It took them less than ten minutes to walk from the Kidron Valley to the Rockefeller Museum, which sat like a mediaeval fortress on the eastern side of the Old City. As Ari had suspected, it was closed to the public. Situated as it was in a Palestinian neighborhood, it did not attract the tourists who instead put the Israel Museum on their must-see list. The Israeli guard on duty did not even ask to see their identity cards, evidently already informed by Pincus as to their arrival. But the man looked them over with unconcealed curiosity as they passed through his guard hut. "Upper level by the water fountain," he said in Hebrew, as they proceeded up the long, curved driveway to the main entrance.

Lily, exhausted from the nervous tension of the recent events, rested on a marble bench in the inner courtyard. "I guess this is where Pincus said to meet him." She listlessly glanced around the courtyard, littered with numerous pillars and antiquities.

"Take a drink. You look wiped out." Ari handed her his canteen.

Lily took a long swallow of cool water, and wiped her mouth with the back of her hand. "What do you think he wants from us?"

Ari closed his eyes and looked upward, as if praying for guidance. With his eyes still closed he asked in a weary voice, "Maybe he simply wants to know how we knew about the bomb in the cave."

"Precisely," Pincus said, as he suddenly appeared near the fountain. His once-red hair, now tinged with grey, made the furrows down his cheeks appear even deeper. "Tell me how you two found yourselves in this particular cave." He crossed his arms across his chest and stared intently in their direction. "Don't tell me about another message from the archangel."

Lily's head snapped up. "Wait a minute. Are you disparaging my special relationship with Michael?"

Pincus softened his stance and moved closer to their bench. "No disrespect, but I can't imagine Michael had anything to do with today's events."

Ari took Lily's hand, exerting enough pressure to warn her to hold back. "Look, it was more like intuition led Lily, I mean us, to check out those burial caves. We had no idea we would find a bomb there."

For the count of about twenty heartbeats Pincus said nothing. "What about the two men in the cave? You told Benny you didn't think they were Palestinians, is that correct?"

"Judging by their accents, I would say Jordanian." Ari gazed at a piece of statuary across the courtyard, a carved Star of David with a cross incised in the middle of it. Lily followed his gaze and her eyes widened in surprise. She squeezed his hand to let him know she saw the same anomaly—a Christian symbol inserted on a Jewish one.

Pincus patiently continued his interrogation. "Did you recognize either of them?"

"No."

"How did you know they would be there today?"

"We didn't know. How could we? We'd never seen them before."

"Did they see you?"

"No, we hid when we heard voices in the entrance."

Pincus leaned on a smooth marble pillar nearby. He took out a pouch of tobacco and filled his pipe. After fiddling with a match for several moments, he drew in smoke, held it and blew out with satisfaction. "Explain to me again, Lily, how you decided to pay a visit to this particular burial cave."

Lily stood up to stretch her legs, which by now were feeling cramped on the stone bench. "I believe I gave your assistant Benny an account of how I encountered Lucifer there earlier." She stopped to gauge Pincus's reaction. Seeing no emotion on his face, good or bad, she continued, "I only saw his shadow but I smelled his scent of death."

"So why go back to such an unpleasant place?" He smiled thinly. "I know it's not in your nature to prevaricate or mislead anyone, is it?"

Lily looked at her hands, then back to the unusual carving of the Star of David. "I sensed Ari's half-brother Reza, had something to do with the cave."

"But you said those two men were Jordanian, not Persian." Pincus stared hard at Ari.

Ari responded cautiously, "The Mahdi Brotherhood has infiltrated every corner of the Muslim world, not just Iran."

"Ari, the last time we spoke, you told me some convoluted story about the Brotherhood blowing up the Golan in order to destroy the Sea of Galilee. No mention of a bomb, especially not in Jerusalem."

"That's pretty much how Reza told it to me." Ari closed his fists. "My brother obviously did not tell me the truth."

Pincus tapped his pipe out on a piece of marble antiquity. "We're finished for now. We'll clean up the cave site and post guards there. The bomb squad is already dismantling what's in the metal container. Ari, I want you to extract every bit of info you can from your brother. I know you don't want anything more to do with him, but we need more details about how they smuggled this bomb into Jerusalem." Pincus glared at the couple without seeming to see them, his eyes as cold as the nearby marble statues.

"Sir," Ari said, the tremor in his voice revealing his concern.

Pincus blinked rapidly before responding. "You have something more to say?"

"Before I make contact with my brother again," he almost spat the word brother, "I need you to do something for me."

Pincus folded his arms and stood his ground in an unyielding posture. "Go on."

"I want you to provide my wife and daughter with an unassailable safe house."

Lily gasped in surprise, and then weakly blurted out, "What's wrong with us staying in Scott's cottage?"

Pincus relaxed his stance and put one hand out in a conciliatory gesture. "I see your point. The place you're staying is no longer safe." He looked with concern at Lily. "I know you don't want to be separated, but it won't be forever. Trust me on that point. The sooner we wrap up this threat and I'm finished with the two of you, the better I can sleep."

Lily moved into Ari's outstretched arms. With a sigh, she laid her head on her husband's shoulder, acknowledging their time together in the little cottage might be over. It had seemed too good to be true. Now they must retrieve Abigail from Scott's keeping and disappear, once again.

Pincus shuffled his feet and cleared his throat. "I'll send you in an unmarked car to pick up your daughter and some of your belongings. I assume, Ari, you plan to stay at his place?"

Ari looked exceedingly unhappy. "I hadn't given it any thought before now. But under the circumstances, I think I should stay there and continue working underground with Scott." He looked deeply into Lily's eyes. "Will I know where the safe house is?"

Pincus reached for his mobile phone. "Not for the time being, for everyone's safety." He proceeded to speak in rapid Hebrew to someone on the other end of his connection. The call lasted less than a minute. "It's all arranged. A van will arrive here after dark. Lily will be reunited with her daughter and driven to an unknown destination. Ari, you will come to my office for further debriefing. Then you will be free to return to the cottage and continue your work with the professor, if you so wish."

Ari offered his hand to Pincus as if to seal the deal. "I'll do my best to gather what information I can from Reza." He didn't use the words thank you, but they were implied in his handshake.

"In the meantime, I'll have the security guard send some lunch up here. You must be famished, as well as exhausted by today's events."

Ari smiled, for the first time that morning. "A falafel stuffed with everything, and two large cokes would not be refused." He kissed Lily's damp cheek and pressed her close.

Chapter 29

The secluded convent, surrounded by a ten-foot stone wall, stood on the edge of a village facing the Jerusalem Forest. Lily had originally been assigned a cottage situated behind the main building, which the French sisters thought would give her more privacy, but Pincus vetoed that idea. "Too dangerous," he'd barked over the phone. "House them snuggly among the nuns, cheek to jowl, so to speak."

The hot, dry *khamsin* weather had blown away, and the air felt crisper, almost cold with a hint of moisture, as if it might rain. Lily felt free to roam the gardens with its small forest of firs and pines. She would have preferred to stay in the private cottage among the fragrant trees, but she said nothing, not knowing how to relate to the sisters she sheltered among. The first week, she ate her meals in her room or on the balcony. But the solitude soon grated on her nerves, and she asked if she and Abigail could eat the main meal in the refectory with the others.

The answer was yes, of course, but it did little to ease her loneliness as the sisters spoke French, and in any case maintained their silence throughout the meal. Nevertheless, they smiled and passed special tidbits along to Abigail, who now ate bits of solid food, like cooked carrots or potatoes.

One afternoon, while they cleared the tables, Lily tried to have a conversation with the head sister, who spoke English and even some Hebrew. "How is it you are on such good terms with Pincus?" She pointedly did not use the word Mossad.

Sister Angelica paused, and then motioned for Lily to follow her onto the patio. The scent of honeysuckle lay heavy in the air. The sister inhaled deeply then tucked her hands into the broad sleeves of her linen robe. "I thought

Monsieur Pincus might have told you about the founder of our sisterhood. She fought in the French underground during the war. Afterward, she gathered a few like-minded women and founded the Sisters of Zion. Their mission was to pray for the Jews and render aid and hospitality when asked."

Lily gave a derisive laugh. "That's what you call atonement?" Lily sat on a wicker chair and set Abigail down to crawl about.

Sister Angelica looked at Lily with the trace of a smile on her lips. "There is one atonement, that of the Lamb of God and he died a Jew."

"Oh," Lily said, taken aback and regretting her bitter tone. Not knowing how to respond, she changed the subject. "Do you often take guests like us who have to stay hidden?"

Sister Angelica laughed in a soft, musical tone. "You are the first in a long time, in fact, the only one during my tenure here."

"How long has that been?"

"Twelve years."

"Do you get homesick for France?" Lily looked straight into the sister's light blue eyes.

"No, we never look back once we take the veil. My home is here." Sister Angelica smiled and spread her arm toward the carefully tended gardens. "Is it not a beautiful place?"

Lily looked happy, if only momentarily, as she surveyed the flowerbeds, the fruit trees, and the gnarled olive trees with their dusky, green leaves.

The sister bent her head, looking in the direction of Abigail crawling on her chubby knees. "Come to evening prayer in the chapel. Listen with your heart." Then she gracefully turned and left the patio.

Later that night, Lily did attend evening prayers after she had put Abigail to bed. She sat in the back pew of the small chapel. The service had already begun, and no one noticed her silent entrance. To her astonishment, the sisters were chanting in Hebrew. Lily recognized Psalm 8, *Oh Lord our God, how excellent is thy name in all the earth.* She silently mouthed the rest of the psalm along with the others. She didn't stay long, not wanting to leave Abigail unattended for more than a few minutes, and slipped out as silently as she had come in.

Back in her comfortably furnished bedroom, she checked on her daughter's breathing, smoothed an unruly tendril off her face, and then sat in the armchair by the French doors. She saw a sprinkling of stars in the sky and wondered if Ari gazed at the same sky. It comforted her to think he did. She knew this safe house was necessary, if only for Abigail's sake, but she didn't like the separation. Still, it was not so bad here with the Sisters of Zion. She had to trust Pincus would not let any harm come to Ari, or Scott, for that matter.

Lily's eyelids closed as sleep overcame her while sitting in the soft chair. Then, for no discernible reason, Lily woke with a start. By now, the moon was glowing high overhead and shining so brightly she could no longer see the stars through the windows. Her nerves were strung taut, like a kite in high wind. She listened intently, turning her head this way and that. No sounds came from inside the convent, but she knew the sisters maintained a strict code of silence, speaking only when necessary.

Lily stealthily opened the French doors without a sound and stepped out onto the balcony. In the distance, a dog howled at the moon, otherwise she heard or saw nothing. She wished she had night vision goggles so she could scan the garden and nearby trees. The cool air caused her to shiver. *What am I doing here?* Turning abruptly back into the bedroom, she changed into her pajamas, and as she still couldn't sleep, she took a seat again in the soft armchair.

Her mind roved over the past, replaying scenes that caused her heart to race. She tried, in vain, to regain the peace she'd felt in the chapel as the sisters chanted so charmingly in Hebrew. *What am I missing? I obeyed my intuition and showed Ari the cave. We stopped a major catastrophe, didn't we?* But that same inner voice told her it was not over yet. More must be done, much more. Only what?

* * * *

Ari stared up into the night sky, observing the milky heat of the stars glistening pinkish white. He sat in a wicker chair in the garden of Scott's house with the silence of the neighborhood strangely comforting. His thoughts turned to Lily, wondering where Pincus had hidden her. Not a sound reached him from the adjoining Arab Girls' School, shut up tight for the night, nor did he hear anything from St. George's School for Boys across the street. A watch dog barked as an occasional vehicle drove through the darkened neighborhood. If any nightlife existed, it wasn't happening in East Jerusalem. Ari knew the restaurants, discos and bars would still be open in West Jerusalem, and pedestrians eating ice cream cones would still be strolling down the Ben Yehuda Mall.

Reluctantly, his thoughts turned to his lengthy debriefing at the Mossad headquarters. It would have been almost comical if the stakes had not been so high. Again, and again, Pincus demanded to know how they knew about the bomb in the Cave of Jehoshaphat. When Ari gave no answer which satisfied him, Pincus had switched topics, his face had turned red, and then pale again, as he badgered him about Reza. How had his brother been involved? Was Ari positive Reza had not been one of the two men in the cave? When had the Mahdi Brotherhood planned to detonate the bomb? What would they do now that it had been discovered? And lastly, asked with evident pain in his voice, could there be another bomb?

After two hours of this, they had released Ari, not even offering him a lift in one of their vehicles, but turned him loose to walk back to Scott's place in the middle of the night.

Unable to sleep, he decided to pay a surprise visit to his brother. Hopefully, at this hour he could evade the minders Pincus had watching him.

It took Ari only minutes to walk the few blocks and slip undetected into the deserted inner courtyard of the American Colony Hotel. The spiky leaves of enormous date palms partially obscured the night sky. To his surprise, he saw Reza, with his hands clasped behind his back, silently treading around the blue-tiled water fountain. Entrenched in his own thoughts, he never heard footsteps approaching.

"Reza," Ari whispered in a tone that did not bode well for brotherly love.

Reza's feet froze in place as if every nerve and cell in his body strained to decipher who had spoken. He waited for the voice to reveal its position.

"It's me." After a long pause fraught with menace, Ari added, "Your brother."

Breathing an audible sigh of relief Reza responded, "*Khoda ashuk*, praise be to God." He stepped forward and threw his arms out as if to embrace Ari, who at the same time took a step backward into the shadows.

"Let's go inside," Ari whispered hoarsely.

"Of course," Reza responded hesitantly, no longer sure of himself.

Ari did not take a seat on the sofa as his brother politely suggested. Instead he stood, facing Reza, who also chose not to sit down. "What is the matter? What brings you here in the middle of the night?"

Ari stared hard at his brother, trying to read his face. "You don't know about the bomb, do you?"

"You are speaking of the one in Damascus, yes?"

Ari grimaced. "Not Damascus, here. You lied to me."

Reza's eyebrows pinched together in bewilderment. "I don't know what you are talking about. A bomb here in Jerusalem?"

"That's right. A nuclear weapon stashed in the Cave of Jehoshaphat."

Reza suddenly sat down on a chair, his right hand over his heart as if he might be having an attack. His face looked pale and clammy. "They never informed me." He looked up at Ari with a mixture of curiosity and awe in his eyes. "But you, being the Mahdi, you know all and see all."

Ari impatiently shook his head. "It's not how you think. But yes, I found their hidden bomb. Now, I want you to find out who in the Brotherhood had the authority and expertise to detonate it."

Chapter 30

Outside it poured for two days, the latter rains of early autumn. Ari and Scott played chess most of the day, sometimes one won, sometimes the other. Time stood still, and now on the third day, the rain stopped, and under a clear blue sky, Ari received a sealed envelope from his brother, the one he had patiently waited for.

That very afternoon, Ari walked east, beyond the city limits to a hilltop surround by tall trees. In the midst of the trees stood what looked like an abandoned monastery, not an unusual happenstance in the Holy Land. The plaster on the walls was peeling, the window panes smashed, red clay shingles were missing from the roof. He let his eyes roam over the dilapidated façade. Curiosity, mingled with trepidation, compelled him to push open the door which hung ajar on rusty hinges.

The musty odor of mice droppings and mold caused him to breathe in shallow gulps. Startled bats swarmed into the upper reaches of the hall when he took the stairs to the second floor, as he had been instructed to do in the message from his brother. On the landing, he had to choose between three closed doors. Two doors were made of pine, faded and scuffed-looking. The door on the right, which would make the room inside face the Temple Mount, appeared to be made out of heavy, dark red cedar.

Ari did not knock, as befitted someone of his status, but turned the old-fashioned door knob, walked in with head held high, shoulders back, and a deliberately sardonic smile on his face. As he had surmised, the tall windows of the large room faced west with a spectacular view of the Al Aqsa mosque in the distance. Standing by a round wooden table stood a lanky, gaunt man, with snow white hair and narrow but clever eyes. He wore an impeccably tailored western suit and no head gear, such as was common among Arab men. With a shrewd glance, Ari noted the man had slim hands with finely shaped fingers, as if they were designed to build delicate bombs.

"*Salaam alechem*," said the man by the table. "It is my honor to meet you at last." He smiled thinly.

"*Alechem salaam*," replied Ari, still standing by the open door.

"Come in and shut the door, bats." He motioned with his arm to a velvet covered chair near the windows, and at the same time introduced himself as Abu Jihad.

Ari walked slowly over to the windows. "You have an excellent view," Ari commented. He remained standing.

The uncomfortable standoff between them was interrupted by a knock on the door, followed by a young boy who held a silver tray with two glasses of hot steaming tea. Ari marveled that somewhere in this ruined monastery, a working kitchen existed. Drinking tea while standing did not seem a desirable option, so Ari reluctantly sat on the ornate velvet chair, while his host pulled a plain wooden one over and sat facing the windows with him, not side by side, but close enough.

Abu Jihad delicately sipped his tea. "I hear the Jews are excavating outside the walls in what they call the City of David. Burrowing like rats underneath the homes of faithful Muslims."

"Is that how the Jews found the bomb hidden in the Cave of Jehoshaphat?" Ari asked, accusing Abu Jihad of possible negligence, trying to throw him off balance.

"The two men involved with that fiasco have been dealt with." Abu Jihad stared off into the distance, his face a mask of indifference.

"To avoid such mistakes in the future, I will require you to keep Reza informed of all your actions. He will then report directly to me," Ari commanded.

Abu Jihad's face showed no expression, although Ari detected a glint of cunning, quickly effaced by dull submission. Boldly taking a chance, Ari decided to act as if he knew a second bomb, a back-up of the original, was part of Abu Jihad's mission.

"There can be no mistakes made with the second bomb." Ari paused to gauge Abu Jihad's response. Seeing no reaction in his dark eyes, which stared back without blinking, he continued, "You will take me to the place where the second weapon is hidden." Ari used all his inner strength to keep his voice from revealing his growing anxiety. How far could he push this white-haired bomb maker, who would gladly die for the cause of destroying Israel? And more to the point, would Pincus have him covered?

Ari thought he detected, if just momentarily, a twitch in Abu Jihad's cheek. The glinting eyes quickly veiled themselves in opaqueness as Abu Jihad stood stiffly at attention. "I am your most humble servant, Your Holiness." He turned and motioned with his arm for Ari to precede him out of the room. "I have a vehicle and driver waiting out back," Abu Jihad murmured, causing Ari to wonder if this wily fox had anticipated such a request from him.

The vehicle sitting in the shade of a pine tree turned out to be an old Mercedes Benz, the model Arab taxi drivers used almost exclusively. Ari grudgingly admitted to himself that this was the perfect way to get around without arousing suspicion. The driver, a middle-aged, nondescript Palestinian with a large mustache and even larger potbelly, sat behind the wheel. He quickly tossed his lit cigarette out the open window and turned off the jazz station when he saw Abu Jihad approach.

Ari accepted the comfort of the back seat, while Abu Jihad took the passenger seat next to the driver. They briefly spoke together in rapid Arabic and then the driver turned on the ignition and smoothly drove away from the derelict monastery heading towards the Mount of Olives. When they reached the top of the ridge, he wondered if they would turn right towards Bethpage, or left onto the road leading to Mount Scopus and the Hebrew University. The driver drove toward the university.

Ari could only hope the second bomb was not planted somewhere on the campus. Beads of sweat appeared on his upper lip as he thought of the casualties such an explosion would produce. Fortunately, only the driver could see this in his rear view mirror and the man seemed too intimidated by his passenger to gaze at Ari. There was little traffic at this time of day, but the road proved narrow, and the driver kept his eyes straight ahead.

With a sense of relief he carefully concealed, Ari watched from the back seat as the driver turned away from the university and drove down the seldom-used lane that led to the village of Isafiya. This small enclave of modest, working-class Palestinian homes clung to the eastern side of Mount Scopus. Ari knew this particular village was infamous for it radical elements, and if Pincus had men following him by car, they would turn back at this juncture. No Israeli would drive through this village and expect to get out alive. He could only hope Pincus had provided air cover, although he could detect no sound of a helicopter.

When the driver came to the end of the village, he turned the Mercedes into the driveway of what appeared to be a warehouse. Using a remote control device on his dashboard, he activated a metal gate and they continued behind the building and out through another gate in the back. Now he drove over a deeply rutted dirt road that meandered down into the *wadi*.

Ari could see nothing but barren hills, covered in a thin layer of fresh vegetation, watered by the recent rains. The sky overhead reflected clear blue, with a few wispy clouds blowing briskly by. Ari had never felt so alone, not even when he had taken the trip to the Sinai had he felt like this. He weighed his options, figuring if they had brought him out here to kill him, he could take out Abu Jihad with his bare hands, snapping the old man's thin neck in one quick jerk. The driver looked much younger, overweight, and probably armed. Ari would have to disable him with a quick jab to his throat before he had time to reach for his weapon.

For no apparent reason Ari could see, the driver abruptly stopped the car. Ari calmed his mind, and prepared himself to strike while at the same time he maintained a faint smile. He opened his door, not waiting for the other two to get out first. Abu Jihad spoke something to the driver and then opened his door, and stepped out. When Ari saw the driver light up a cigarette, he mentally let down his guard, but still kept his eyes on Abu Jihad.

"This way, if you please," The old man said as he carefully picked his way among the rocks and boulders that covered the bottom of the *wadi*. He laughed harshly. "If there should be a flash flood farther up the riverbed we are doomed."

Ari grunted an acknowledgement. He knew only too well the danger of hiking where a flash flood could occur at any time. He mentally gauged the angle of the ravine, estimating how fast he could run if it became necessary.

He estimated he could sprint to higher elevation, but Abu Jihad could not. *So be it*, he thought grimly. He once again scanned the sky, hoping to see an aircraft. All he saw was the dark wingspan of a *nesher*, an eagle, gracefully sweeping on the downdrafts.

The dry river bed brought to Ari's mind the story of Elijah, the biblical prophet who had hidden in this very area of Wadi Kelt, drinking from the stream and eating food the ravens dropped in his camp. Unlike the eagle overhead, ravens were scavengers, and likely left rotten meat for Elijah's consumption. Ari shook his head acknowledging when it came to survival, anything would do. He must survive at all cost, not just for himself, but for the sake of the others who would die if a nuclear weapon were detonated. His thoughts turned to Lily and Abigail, and for the first time, he hoped and prayed Pincus had sent them to a safe house outside Israel.

Walking behind Abu Jihad, who picked his way among the boulders and rocks as if he had done this many times before, Ari found they were now on a narrow path, perhaps made by goats, which led up the incline of the river bed. They stopped to catch their breath, and while staring out at the Judean wilderness, Ari once again saw the shadow of the eagle's wings on the ground as it swooped in for a kill. Abu Jihad's expression looked grim as he pointed to a thorn bush precariously growing out of the rocky hillside. "Just there, behind the bush."

"After you," Ari murmured. He followed as they entered a narrow cleft that soon opened into a cavern as large as a room in a house. The smell hit him first, musty and rich with animal droppings. Ari's eyes slowly adjusted to the semi-darkness of the cave, while Abu Jihad walked as surefooted as a deer.

"Here." Abu Jihad pointed to a dark corner, "The back-up bomb." He handed Ari a flashlight.

Ari felt his throat go dry as fear sped through his system like poison. He swallowed once and then again. What was the plan he and Pincus had agreed upon? His mind blankly scrambled for an answer to the terror which lay in the dark corner. After what seemed like an eternity to Ari's frozen brain, he could only think to ask what might be construed as a foolish question.

"Why did you inform my brother Reza the bombs were hidden in Damascus, waiting to be transported to the Golan? Why did Reza believe you wanted to create an earthquake to destroy the Sea of Galilee?"

Abu Jihad turned and faced Ari. In the dim light, Ari could not see his demeanor nor did he want to shine his flashlight directly into the old man's eyes. The atmosphere in the cave created the illusion of timelessness. Past, present and future melded into a moment of consciousness that left Ari breathless, but strangely no longer afraid.

"Your Holiness, I am not pleased to be the one to say it, but Reza is not to be trusted. We in the Brotherhood thought it best to misdirect him." Abu Jihad stood absolutely still, breathing as shallowly as humanly possible. He continued speaking when Ari made no comment. "Reza came under interrogation of the Mossad, as you are aware. After that, we could never be sure if he had not been turned into a double agent."

"My own brother?" Ari asked, incredulously. "You think I wouldn't know if he were a traitor?"

Abu Jihad coughed nervously. "We had to be sure. We gave him orders to kill even you, knowing that as the Mahdi, you have the power of resurrection. This was the ultimate test of his loyalty to our cause."

"What is your plan now?" Ari asked, desperately playing for time and hoping against hope Pincus and his team would show up any minute.

"It is for you to set the time and date for the destruction of the Mount of Olives. When this bomb is detonated, the two mountains will be cleft in two. Mount Scopus and the Mount of Olives will be leveled. Then the world will know your time has come. Your Holiness, the Mahdi, will bring peace and security to the Middle East."

Once again, Ari felt the moisture in his mouth dry up and his throat closed. He did not know how or what to answer to such madness. The burden weighing upon him felt too much to bear.

Chapter 31

Later that night, Ari returned to the cottage on Scott's property. He had left Abu Jihad with firm instructions to do nothing about the bomb until further notice. Ari had implied, but not explicitly stated, that he would deal with Reza himself. At this juncture, Ari didn't know what to think, although he wanted to believe Reza would not betray him.

Exhaustion, both mental and physical set in before he had the chance to take off his boots. He sat on a stool, staring at the wall when he heard a knock on the door. Wishing it might be his beloved Lily, but knowing she would never be allowed to return to this place, he focused his eyes and willed himself to respond in as strong a voice as he could muster. "Come in, it's not locked."

Expecting Scott to show his face, Ari momentarily felt off balance by the entrance of Motti Pincus, the last person he wanted to see just now.

"Good evening," Pincus said, as he took a chair and sat facing Ari. "Nice little place you have here." His gaze slowly took in the simply furnished room. "Did you have a successful little *tiyul* in the *wadi*?"

Ari's eyes burned with resentment which he quickly hid with sarcasm. "Like you care, and where were you today?" Ari wished now he hadn't quit smoking. A cigarette would calm his nerves, as well as hide his agitation as he lit up and inhaled. Even as he thought about such devious tactics, he wondered how Pincus knew where he had been.

"Maybe your men followed me as far as the village of Isafiya, but I saw no sign of them when Abu Jihad took me down into the dry river bed." Ari snorted with disgust.

"Is that what he calls himself these days, Abu Jihad?" Pincus almost smiled. "We know him by another name, but that's not important. What did the silver fox, as we fondly call him, have up his sleeve, another bomb perhaps?"

"All right, so you know this guy and how he makes a living. So, knowing how dangerous he is, why did you let him take me so far into the wilderness? What about my backup?"

Pincus scrutinized his fingernails, picking at an imaginary hangnail before responding. "First, there were only two men, one very old, and the other very fat. We figured you could handle the situation if necessary."

Ari wanted to smile, secretly pleased the Mossad thought him so capable. His army training had been thorough, but it had been a long time ago.

Pincus took no notice of Ari and continued speaking. "We had you covered all the way. Happen to notice an eagle?"

"That was you?" Ari's jaw dropped. Quickly recovering, he asked, "A remote-controlled drone?"

Pincus narrowed his eyes and nodded. "Of course, but we couldn't see what you found inside the cave, now could we?"

Ari's tense muscles visibly relaxed as his shoulders dropped in relief knowing Pincus had not let him down. His voice trembled with emotion as he related what he'd found in the cave. Pincus heard him out with a grave expression on his face.

"Well, Ari, we can handle the dismantling of another bomb. But it won't be easy for you to explain to the Mahdi people how we found it. Abu Jihad will surely arrange to eliminate both you and Reza."

"I think he's already come to that conclusion. The only reason I'm still alive is that he fears I have occult powers that allow me to never die."

"How convenient, for you," Pincus said dryly. "Nevertheless, I believe you are mortal, and therefore, we are sending you and your family out of Israel for the time being." Pincus stood up to indicate the discussion finished.

"Wait a minute. What if I don't agree with your plan? Have you said anything to Lily?" In his agitation Ari nearly tipped over the table.

Pincus put out one hand to steady it. "You have no choice in the matter. But it will take some time to create entirely new identities for the three of you. In the meantime, you will remain here under Scott's kind hospitality. Lily and Abigail will stay where they are in the safe house."

Reluctantly, Ari followed his visitor out the door, desperate to not let him go without further explanations. "What do I tell Scott in the meantime?"

"We have thoroughly vetted him. You can tell him as much or little as you deem prudent. Naturally, we will keep round-the-clock surveillance on the both of you."

Before Ari could react to this bit of information, Pincus disappeared through a back gate, and into a waiting car. Puzzled, Ari stared at the gate he had thought permanently locked, facing as it did the ultra-orthodox neighborhood of Mea Sharim. Turning back towards the main house, he decided to wake Scott and find out how much he already knew.

Ari pounded heavily on the kitchen door until a disgruntled Scott appeared, yawning and blinking his eyes. "What do you need at this hour?" Scott asked, plainly irritated at having been awakened from deep sleep.

"Let's talk inside." Ari pushed his way past Scott and stood by the sink. "Maybe you can make some coffee?"

Scott scratched his head. "Of course, Ari."

When the water boiled, and the rich aroma of Turkish coffee filled the room, the two men sat and faced each other.

"Let me begin with a question." Ari now felt somewhat contrite at having disturbed his friend's sleep. "Who else has a key to that back gate?"

"What do you mean who else? Even I don't have a key. Someone lost it decades ago and never replaced it. Or so they told me when I leased this place."

"Evidently, the Mossad has a key. Pincus just paid me a visit." Ari stared at Scott to gauge his reaction, and he thought Scott not sufficiently surprised.

"Ari, I don't pretend to understand what you do. I offered Lily and you a place to stay. I even offered you work, so you could stay out of sight for the time being. What business you have with Pincus is not my concern."

Ari drank his coffee to the dregs, put down his cup, and softened his tone of voice. "I know, and I appreciate all you've done. I suppose I'm somewhat rattled by his surprise visit. The Mossad knows all about you, by the way."

"That doesn't surprise me." Scott smiled. "I chose to work in an unstable neighborhood, didn't I?"

Ari laughed bitterly. "You don't know the half of it."

"Tell me," Scott replied. "But only if you want to."

"You know about the bomb we found in the Cave of Jehoshaphat, right?" He didn't wait for an answer. "Today I found another one hidden in the wilderness behind Mount Scopus."

"What do you mean *found*? Just out hiking and you stumbled on it?"

"No, I was taken there by a member of the Mahdi Brotherhood. It's a complicated story, but the end results are Lily, Abigail, and I will be sent abroad. I will stay here with you until Pincus can arrange the details of our new identities. You know passports, birth certificates, and a fake history." Ari grimaced in distaste.

"In the meantime, I assume you and I will be safe here?" Scott frowned unhappily.

Ari shrugged. "I just don't know. I can't make any promises."

Scott briskly picked up the used coffee cups and rinsed them in the sink. "If people can come and go as they please on this property, as Pincus just did, then I suggest you sleep here in the big house." Over Ari's vehement protest, Scott insisted on making up a bed in one of the rooms set aside for the volunteer students who never seemed to arrive.

Ari reluctantly acquiesced, and when the lights went out, and stillness hung in the cool night air, he sat on the end of the cot and thought about the future for Lily, Abigail, and himself. They couldn't go on this way. As he mentally conjured up a picture of his daughter's curly hair, big brown eyes, and laughing mouth, he remembered, with a sharp pang in his chest, the lion-shaped birthmark on her tiny shoulder, *the birthmark that resembles the one on my cheek—the mark of the Mahdi.*

Chapter 32

Tranquility dominated the atmosphere of the convent, but Lily's mind churned with schemes of how to extract herself from the watchful care of the Mossad. She would not let Pincus orchestrate their future, no matter how well-intentioned his plans. Living under assumed names in another country was not how she wanted Abigail's childhood to unfold. But she needed advice and the only ones she trusted to give good counsel were the two brothers, Dan and Eli.

First, she thought she might slip out the gate while the sisters were busy going about their chores. This was not a prison. But someone had to watch Abigail. So, this morning she confided in Sister Angelica. She told the unsuspecting nun she needed just a few hours to gather up some of her personal effects she had left with friends in the Old City.

"Three hours tops. If you could ask one of the sisters to babysit, I would be grateful," Lily pleaded.

Sister Angelica showed no emotion when she heard the request, instead she asked the obvious question. "Is it safe for you to leave here? Won't you be recognized by the people who want to harm you?"

"Not if you loan me a robe and veil. Dressed as a nun, I can move about freely." Lily tilted her head and smiled in her most beguiling manner. "I can be back before lunch if I leave now."

* * * *

Dressed in a tan linen robe, Lily boarded a bus that delivered her to the central station. In the terminal, she went into the ladies restroom dressed as a nun and walked out a few minutes later in her own clothes, the habit stuffed into a shopping bag. Then she boarded another bus to Jaffa Gate. Walking briskly, she covered the short distance to the Armenian Quarter and Dan and Eli's apartment.

She knew she risked they would not be home, but the weight of her anxiety about the future propelled her to take the chance. With a sigh of relief, she heard someone coming down the stairs to answer the bell.

"Lily, what a surprise." Dan shook his mop of black curls peppered with grey. His wide smooth forehead wrinkled with a puzzled look.

She followed Dan up the stairs to the second floor landing, and he ushered her inside with a flourish. After she made herself comfortable on the sofa, Dan sat down opposite her and looked expectantly in her direction. "*Nu*, so? What brings you here this morning? Don't tell me it's a social call. We both know it's not your style."

Lily laughed. "Nor yours." She adjusted the hem of her sleeve as a delaying tactic before continuing. "Is your brother home?"

"Eli is upstairs in the prayer room." He looked piercingly at Lily. "Do you want me to get him?"

"Not yet. I suppose I can tell you why I came," she said modestly, still buying time.

"I'm guessing you want advice, right?"

Lily smiled ruefully. "Ari and I always seem to be in some kind of dilemma, don't we?"

Dan said nothing, but stood and went to the kitchen to put on the kettle. He returned with a tray holding a coffee pot and a plate of cookies. He set it down and sat facing Lily again. "My brother and I were expecting you to visit, you know."

Lily's eyes widened. "You were?" To hide her nervousness, she reached for a cookie and took a bite, although she didn't feel the least bit hungry.

Dan poured them each a cup from the pot. "We've been thinking a lot about you and Ari in recent days." He paused to take a sip. "You're in real danger, aren't you?"

Ignoring her coffee, Lily looked straight into Dan's face. "You won't believe what we've just been through. I'm sorry but I can't tell you any of the details."

"I know, state secrets," Dan replied.

Just then Eli walked in the door. "What's this about keeping secrets?" He smiled, obviously pleased to see Lily sitting there. This short, genial-looking man with soulful brown eyes still wore his hair cut in a bowl shape like a monk's.

"I was telling Dan about the difficult time Ari and I have just gone through, only I can't reveal any of it." Lily felt distressed enough to cry.

"So, tell us what you can," Eli said with brisk solicitude.

Lily blurted out the essence of the problem: she and Abigail were in a Mossad safe house, and Ari remained with Professor Scott, waiting for Pincus to arrange their transfer abroad.

"I can't live my life this way. It is not who we are, Ari and I. You know?" She sniffed and wiped away a tear which fell unbidden on her cheek.

Eli responded first. "We understand. God has a different plan for the two of you." He thought a moment and then added, "And of course, Abigail."

Dan nodded in agreement. "We spoke about your being a part of the restoration of the fallen tabernacle of David, remember?"

"Well, yes. I vaguely remember something about the tent of David. But what does it mean in practical terms, because we're going to be shipped out of here very soon."

"Well," Eli said softly, "I can't give you exact details. We don't understand all the implications ourselves. You and Ari must trust God to show you what to do next."

"What my brother isn't telling you is that we've had recent visions and dreams to indicate some kind of catastrophe is about to happen. What and when?" He opened the palms of both hands indicating he did not have the answer.

"We recently defused such a catastrophe," Lily exclaimed. "I'm not supposed to talk about it, but I can tell you a nuclear threat has been averted."

Dan shared a grave look with his brother. "That may be so, but the danger we speak of has not passed. It is still to happen."

"A second bomb," Lily mumbled. "I need to get in touch with Ari." She started to get up when Eli motioned for her to stay seated.

"Our interpretation of the vision leans toward a natural disaster, a force of nature perhaps." Eli poured himself some coffee before continuing. "My brother and I have recently come into a modest inheritance." He paused and brought the cup to his lips. "My uncle died and left us his holdings in the Negev, a small ranch with several barns and cottages."

Dan interjected, "What some people might call a kibbutz or commune. It's been derelict and uninhabited for years. Lack of water, lack of interested people, you get the picture."

Lily blinked with incomprehension. "Mazel tov on your inheritance, but what does this have to do with Ari and me?"

"We're moving there and plan to build a community of believers in the Negev. It will be called Bet Abraham." Eli looked intently at his hands and then back to Lily.

Dan then added, "Our piece of land is located between Beer Sheva and Hebron in the plains of Mamre. Does that ring a bell?" When Lily shook her head he continued, "Abraham pitched his tent there."

"Oh, I see," Lily said, even though she didn't see.

Dan, intuiting the discussion had reached its limit, stood and gently walked Lily to the door. "We are going there to prepare a place of refuge, so to speak. You and your family will always be welcome."

* * * *

Lily returned to the convent the same way she came, changing her clothing in the restroom of the bus station. Safely back behind the convent walls, she contacted Pincus and warned him there might be a second bomb. He did not sound surprised by her news which puzzled her. She made no mention of the possibility of a natural disaster. And she did not tell Pincus about Bet Abraham in the Negev. This would be her secret, and she would not tell Ari until she understood what it meant. Could she live in the Negev? Was this even a halfway viable option? Could they rely on Dan and Eli? She needed answers, now. The time had come to consult the *urim* and *thummin* stones!

Abigail quietly napped on the bed, as Lily pulled out the small velvet pouch she wore around her neck. With a casual indifference which belied her sense of urgency, she tossed the stones onto the bedspread. One was black and shiny as a pearl, and the other milky white. The very stones she had found in a cave, erroneously thinking she had discovered the tomb of King David. She stared at them for a long moment, wondering how two such inanimate objects could hold such power. It had been a long time since she had consulted the wisdom of the *urim* and *thummin*, and her entire body trembled as she picked up the smooth stones, caressing them with her fingers, delighting in the silky, smooth texture. She glanced over at the sleeping form of her daughter. Without further ado, Lily slipped the stones back in the tiny, velvet pouch, and shook it gently to redistribute their position relative to each other. Then she tightly closed her eyes, took a deep breath and asked the question troubling her.

"Should we go south, and hide in the Negev?" Lily asked in a soft, but clear voice. She thrust her hand in the pouch and touched one of the stones. Both stones were identical in shape and texture, so she could not choose the white over the black, even if she wanted to. When she withdrew her fingers, she saw she was holding the luminescent white stone, the one that signified a positive answer, a yes. Her heart skipped a beat as she weighed the importance of the affirmative answer. The Negev was a dry wasteland. As far as she knew, few towns or settlements had thrived there since the beginning of the State of Israel, Be'er Sheva being one of the exceptions. Then she couldn't ignore the fact that Ari had been born somewhere in the Negev, tossed away at birth in some desolate immigrant town, where hope was as scarce as water, housing, or employment. It was madness to consider taking Abigail there. There must be something wrong with how she approached the selection of the white stone.

Lily quickly tossed the stone back in the velvet sack, gave it a good shake and repeated her question. Her cheeks burned when the same pale stone appeared once again in her fingers. Ashamed at herself for doubting the leading of the *Shikinah*, she bowed her head in contrition. "Dear God of Abraham, Isaac, and Jacob, I will go to the Negev, to this kibbutz of the brothers. Help me to convince Ari. Amen." She kept her eyes closed and murmured for the first time in her life, "In the name of Yeshua Ha Mashiach."

Chapter 33

Standing underground in a natural cave, Ari listened to Scott's lecture on the geographical layout of Jerusalem in ancient times. "You probably are not aware that Jerusalem was built on four hills. At that time Mt. Zion, which is situated southwest of where we stand, was higher than mount Moriah."

Scott pulled out a heavily creased map. "See, here's what the original Mt. Zion looked like, and you can see the elevation is higher than Mount Moriah."

"I always thought the temple mount was the highest point." Ari directed his flashlight on the old map and stared intently.

"No, Ari, history records when the Greeks occupied Jerusalem they built their fortress on Mt. Zion, where they could deliberately dominate the Jewish temple and thus disturb the worshipers. When the Maccabees got the upper hand, they wiped away all trace of the Greeks by demolishing their fortress and leveling Mt. Zion to a pile of rubble. No longer would any foreign power look down on the temple."

"Right, so what's the relevance of that to what we're looking for today?" Ari folded and handed the map back to Scott.

"Nothing, really, just a bit of interesting history, but in answer to your question, what we're looking for today are some artifacts dating to the Iron Age habitation."

"I thought you were strictly a pollen man," Ari said tersely.

"Yes, I am that, but if we're lucky enough to find pottery or coins which can be dated, it enables me to better date the pollen I'm extracting."

"So, show me where to core for a sample." Ari pulled the six-inch metal corer from his backpack.

Scott ran his fingers over a smooth portion of the wall nearest him. "Try here. Go in for a depth of three or four inches."

Both men worked without talking for a length of time before Scott broke the silence. "Do you have any idea where the Mossad will relocate you?"

Before replying, Ari paused, carefully pulled his coring device out of the soft limestone, and deposited the soil sample in a sterile envelope. "I have no idea. And I have no choice in the matter. Pincus makes the decisions."

"And you can live with his choice?" Scott looked intently at him.

Ari sighed then coughed as he took in a gulp of the fetid air in the dank cavern. "I've had to live with far worse scenarios these past few years." He held up the coring instrument. "Where should I take the next sample?" He effectively changed the subject.

"Try down here near the floor," Scott said, and then added, "I don't mean to pry, but I'm worried about your little family. I've grown fond of the three of you."

Squatting on his heels, Ari screwed the steel implement deep into the side of the wall just above floor level. With a grunt he pulled it out with a good-size sample enclosed. "I know you mean well. It's just that I don't know which way to go. I grew up believing I was half Jewish and half Palestinian." He gave a bitter laugh of amusement. "If I thought that was a tough combination, it was nothing to finding out the truth. Not only am I of Persian descent on my father's side, but I have the dubious distinction of being their freaking Mahdi."

Scott laid down his tools on a piece of canvas. "You don't have to accept their offer, you know."

Ari's voice rose in anger. "Whose offer, The Mossad's or the Brotherhood's?"

Scott thoughtfully scratched his beard before replying. "Well, you can refuse them both, can't you?"

Ari opened his mouth to reply when he felt a trickle of sand fall on his face. He wiped it away before it got into his eyes just as the floor of the cavern began undulating in waves. He automatically reached out his arm to steady himself against the nearest wall. "What's happening?"

"Let's get out of here," Scott shouted, as he raced for the tunnel leading to the upper level. With Ari right behind, they ran up to the next level of the underground excavations only to find the exit blocked by a landslide of dirt and rubble. A sound like the roar of the ocean vibrated in their ears as the earth beneath their feet kept moving.

"This is a big one," Scott muttered in an awestruck tone of voice. "We need to get under an archway."

They frantically looked around as they dodged falling debris and small boulders. Ari, more agile, with sharper eyesight, and the only one still wearing a headlamp, spotted what looked like a man-made niche carved into the limestone. Together, they crouched under its marble lintel with their hands covering their necks as they waited for the earthquake to pass.

Great convulsions undulated through the subterranean cavern for what seemed like an eternity to the two men trapped below the surface of the earth. Ari was the first to notice the water rising above his ankles and rapidly moving up his calves. "Scott," he whispered in a terrified voice, "We need to get out of here, now."

Scott shoved his hand into the cold water to assess the depth and strength of the current. He quickly pulled it out with a shout of excitement. "This is a new river flowing through here. I have to take measurements and record this."

Ari responded in an equally excited voice, "Who cares if it's a new or old river. We're going to drown if we don't get out!"

"I see your point. But unfortunately, our only exit is collapsed under a ton of rocks and debris. What do you suggest we do?" Scott turned his head, scanning their immediate vicinity.

"Do you have a rock pick in your backpack?" Ari's was voice now deadly calm.

Scott twisted around until he retrieved the sodden pack. "Take it," he said, handing the tool to Ari.

His hands shook from the cold as the water continued to steadily rise, but Ari focused his mind on the task at hand. "I'm going to hack through this wall, or die trying."

Ari drove the pick axe into the soft limestone over and over as Scott crouched beside him and scrabbled through the rubble with his bare hands. The water continued to rise to waist level, but then seemed to stabilize at that point.

"Ari," Scott spoke in a hoarse whisper, "I think this river has reached its natural level. It must be flowing out somewhere."

Ari grunted in acknowledgment and kept pounding the pick into the wall. "I've made a small opening but not big enough to crawl through. Any idea what's on the other side?"

"No idea at all. The maps I have don't indicate any caves there, natural or manmade."

"I smell a difference in the air coming through this opening. There's something there on the other side of this wall. I'm sure of it." With a burst of energy fueled by adrenaline, Ari furiously tore at the earth.

The professor leaned wearily against the side of the cave and spoke in a thin voice etched with fear. "I didn't tell anybody where we would be today, did you?"

"No," Ari replied curtly. "Looks like we're on our own."

"No one's coming to the rescue, you say?"

"Right." Ari continued with the pick axe. "Unless Pincus had me followed, and one of his men might know where we are."

Scott responded, "That's the good news. The bad news is if this has been a major earthquake, they have more to deal with in Jerusalem then two missing archaeologists."

Ominous silence surrounded them in the cold, black underground passage. The only sound was from Ari's axe smashing through the earthen wall as he widened the hole. He shone his headlamp into the aperture but could see nothing. Then he thrust his arm through and was surprised to find cool, dry air. "It feels different on the other side."

"What do you mean, different?" Scott asked in a sharp tone.

"Well, just different. Where we're standing the air is cold and damp. The other side feels warmer."

Scott pulled himself up to his full height, shook his head as if to clear the fog from his mind, and pulled out the small notebook he carried in his shirt pocket. He retrieved a pencil stub from another pocket and recorded their immediate coordinates. "Can't you dig faster?"

Ari turned and scowled at the professor. "I'm doing the best I can, sir." He renewed his efforts by sheer will power, as if to spite Scott. After ten minutes of furious labor, he was able to get his head and one shoulder into the opening. "Shove me through," he called back to Scott. By twisting and turning, Ari barely managed to squeeze his body to the other side.

Scott tried to push through but couldn't make it. "What do you see?"

"Holy Moses," Ari murmured in response. He stood frozen as he stared at the gold-covered sarcophagus standing in the center of the small cave. The earthquake seemed to have bypassed this particular space, as far as Ari could make out. There was no rock debris, and more importantly, no water. In fact, the air in this cave was strangely warm and dry. Ari took a deep breath and filled his lungs with the good, clean air. "Cedar of Lebanon."

"What's that?" Scott shouted from the other side of the opening.

"Smells like the cedars of Lebanon in here, and you won't believe what I'm staring at."

Ari turned when he heard Scott panting as he struggled to squirm though the opening. "Give me a hand," Scott muttered. Ari pulled as Scott twisted, and they managed to get him through in one piece. When Scott recovered his breath, and shook the dirt out of his hair and eyes, he froze in place, as Ari had, as he stared in awe at the magnificent sarcophagus.

Ari broke the silence with a discreet cough. "Maybe a king's resting place?"

Scott again pulled out his pocket-size notebook and began to describe the object in small, tight handwriting. "What do you estimate the dimensions are? Sadly, my measuring tape is in my backpack. And I'm not squeezing through there again."

Ari cautiously stepped closer to the ancient coffin and spread his arms to measure the length. Then he moved to the end and measured the depth. "About the size of an average man, wouldn't you say?"

"No average man's bones lie here. This is obviously the burial site of someone of importance, possibly a king."

Scott methodically wrote more in his notebook. "Now, what did I hear you mumble, something about cedars of Lebanon?"

Ari again inhaled deeply and smiled reflexively. "Can't you smell it? Like incense or something."

Scott breathed in and held his breath before exhaling slowly. Then he carefully scanned the low ceiling and walls. "It looks like this cave has been sealed up for centuries, perhaps millennia."

Ari shook his head in wonderment. "Then where does the fragrance come from? And what explains the warm, dry air?" Ari touched his trousers which already felt drier.

Scott took the few steps to the coffin and gently ran his fingers over the lid. "Note the shiny color of this gold-plate. It should appear dull after so much time has elapsed. It's as if this cave is in a time capsule."

At the mention of the word time, Ari blinked his eyes and remembered where they were and what condition they were in. There appeared to be no way out from this cave, and the passage behind the hole in the wall held no exit either. The air quality was more than good, and there was no danger from drowning, but how long could they survive if no help came? His heart sank in despair, and then he thought of Lily and Abigail. *Oh God, let them be safe. How much of Jerusalem was effected by the earthquake? Were they even in Jerusalem?* He silently made a vow that if he made it out and found his family safe, he would devote the rest of his life to their wellbeing. This would be his answer to the Mossad, and this would be his answer to the Mahdi Brotherhood.

Ari leaned against the wall of the cave and smiled to himself as he watched Scott write page after page in his little notebook. "If we make it out of here, I want nothing more than to settle down with my family, and live safe and secure under our own fig tree, as the saying goes."

Distracted in his thoughts, Scott lifted his head and mumbled, "What's that about fig trees? And could you give me your headlamp? I can barely make out my own handwriting in this dim light." Scott pulled a dun-colored compass out of his pocket, flipped the lid open, and attempted to determine the precise coordinates of this strange cave. The needle fluctuated wildly, stopping nowhere. Scott frowned, smacked the device against his thigh and tried again. "I can't get a reading. There must be unknown mineral deposits here throwing the compass off true north." He then turned the compass on its side in an attempt to record the angle to the ceiling.

Ari shook his head and squatted in a more comfortable position. "There's more than one strange thing going on here. What do you think causes the warm, dry air, or the smell of cedar?"

Scott carefully put his notebook and compass back in his pocket and methodically scanned the cave from top to bottom. He used the tip of his boot to scratch the surface of the dirt floor, and in doing so uncovered a patch of blush-pink marble. "Here's the answer to one of your questions. I suspect this entire space is paved with this type of marble. That would explain the moderate, dry temperature in here."

In response, Ari retrieved the knife he wore in a leg holster, and scrapped at the section nearest him. "You may be right, but what explains the fragrance?"

"Incense," Scott replied. "We've got a royal tomb here, if I'm not mistaken, possibly that of King David. You know, it has never been found."

Ari whistled softly in awe. "Wouldn't Lily like to see this? Remember, she found that burial cave in the monastery garden. She hoped it was King David's tomb, but there was no coffin, no bones. You recall she did find a small, marble box with some artifacts that possibly date back to the time of Aaron, the high priest."

Scott agreed Lily would love to see this. Then he looked at his watch. "We've been underground for more than an hour. If there's a search party, they should have found us by now."

Chapter 34

On the outskirts of Jerusalem, Lily experienced a violent rolling as if she were on a ship. The floor beneath her feet trembled, and the walls swayed for more than ten seconds. She knew something terrible had occurred when Sister Angelica took a call from the mother house in the Old City. In a voice trembling with emotion, the head sister reported to those in the sitting room their sister house on the Via Dolorosa had been leveled by violent tremors registering 6.5 on the Richter scale. Many people were dead or missing.

As the sisters listened in stunned horror, making signs of the cross and crying, Lily turned on the small television in the guest room. She felt her face pale as she watched footage of the destruction. East Jerusalem took the brunt of the quake, which toppled half of the Mount of Olives into the ravine which separated it from Mount Scopus. Her eyes widened in shock as she viewed the military helicopter as it hovered above the Temple Mount. The Al Aqsa mosque was no more. But the famous golden dome which dominated the scene for centuries appeared undamaged. Then the helicopter flew over the Rockefeller Museum which also seemed to have survived untouched by the quake.

"Oh my God," Lily gasped, "Where's Ari?" She stared at the screen as the chopper flew over other landmarks destroyed or no longer recognizable. She thought she heard the newscaster say the American Colony Hotel was heavily damaged. The Intercontinental Hotel on the Mount of Olives was another property in the direct path of the earthquake. Hundreds of tourists were presumed dead. Lily fervently hoped Ari had joined Scott in the City of David, where the caves and caverns would provide shelter.

Sister Angelica ordered the sisters to start gathering first aid supplies, food, water, and blankets. "I'll drive the van as close as I can get to Damascus Gate, and we'll go in by foot. We must help our sisters."

Lily gave Angelica a quick sidewise glance. "I'm going with you. I have to find my husband."

"What about your child?" She shot a pointed glance at Abigail, who by now had begun to wail as she held out her arms to be picked up.

"She'll be safer here with the kitchen staff." Lily comforted her daughter with kisses.

"Yes, yes," Angelica murmured distractedly. "Let's go quickly."

Within an hour, they had packed the old VW van with food, water, and bandages, and drove off with Sister Angelica at the wheel. Parts of the city were untouched by the natural disaster, including the Knesset Building. But the streets were clogged with emergency response vehicles, and hundreds of private citizens trying to leave Jerusalem, or like the nuns, trying to find their loved ones.

Lily asked if any of the sisters in the van had a mobile phone with them. They did not.

"Neither do I, and neither does Ari, but I thought if I had a phone I might get ahold of Professor Scott." Lily faltered. "I don't know what to do."

Silence filled the van as the others fidgeted nervously with their rosary beads. "It will be well with your husband," Angelica observed reflectively.

"How do you know?" Lily asked.

"I can't explain it. I just know."

Lily said nothing as the van traveled through the back streets of Jerusalem. Due to Angelica's careful driving, which involved negotiating many narrow lanes Lily never knew even existed, they found themselves behind the

Rockefeller Museum. It was obvious they could go no further, and here they unloaded the van. Carrying what they could, they started out on foot for the Via Dolorosa.

"Ladies, I'm going to search for Ari. I'll see you back at the convent tonight." Lily turned and headed towards Nablus Road. Some shops lining the avenue were intact, while others looked like they had been bombed out. Shopkeepers hovered in perplexed groups speaking quietly in Arabic. No one paid any attention to the lone woman striding down the middle of the street.

When she reached the vicinity of the American Colony Hotel she paused and stared at what remained of what had been a beautiful, garden paradise. Rescue teams were digging through the debris. Disheveled hotel guests, some only partially clothed, wandered around in a daze. Lily immediately thought of Ari's brother, Reza. She grimaced in distaste. He had an entire suite here. Was he alive? Shaking her head, not willing to find out, she hurried a few streets over to Scott's house.

She drew a deep breath of relief when she saw it still standing, even though the Arab Girls' School next door had sustained considerable damage. Thankfully, the girls were alive, though running around in confusion.

Lily let herself in the front gate and proceeded around the main house to the cottage in the back. Not finding Ari, she ran to the big house, calling his name, but found the house empty. Sitting on a kitchen chair to catch her breath, she looked up and her gaze fell on the wall phone. She quickly got up and dialed the number Pincus had given her for emergencies. If ever there was one, it was now, she decided grimly, ignoring her vow to never again ask him for help. She let the phone ring on and on, but got no answer.

As a last resort, Lily decided to pray. With her eyes wide open she began to address the Almighty, *HaShem,* the name, as commonly used by religious Jews. "And also, Michael, if you are listening," she said reflectively. "Please keep Ari and Scott safe, and help me find them." Since it had been ages since the archangel had appeared to her in person, she thought she might have outgrown the need for the supernatural. Communicating with the archangel had landed her in big trouble in the past, as those in authority had deemed her temporarily insane. Ari no longer doubted this gift, but she knew Scott was skeptical. And Pincus and his team thought it was a joke. Nevertheless, the results of listening to Michael had proved very beneficial when she had thwarted more than one major terrorist attack on Israel.

But now, the need for Michael's intervention was personal—Ari's life hung in the balance. Deep in her gut, she felt he was still alive but trapped somewhere beneath the surface. She sat with her hands in her lap, deliberately slowing her breathing down until her heart pumped slow and steady. The minutes passed with no response from either *HaShem* or the archangel. Lily stood and walked about the room assuming her position made no difference to the Almighty. Getting no response, she pressed her lips together and hummed a little tune. Now fully exasperated, she stopped mindlessly humming and turned her thoughts toward Yeshua. She remembered Dan and Eli prefaced his name with the title Lord. *Maybe, I should ask him. Why not?* She smiled in spite of herself. So she began her request. "*Adon Yeshua,* send help to Ari and Scott, wherever they are."

A gentle breeze blew in from the open window, stirring her hair. At the same time a quiet sense of peace replaced the anxiety and fear which had previously assaulted her emotions. In this state of mind, she whispered eagerly, "Speak Lord, I'm listening."

Lily cocked her head to the side, as if to hear. She remained in that stance for some moments until an interior voice spoke clearly and distinctly, *the scarlet thread.* Although she remained in a state of respectful expectation, no further word or message came. She gradually became aware of the outside noises, as sirens blared in the congested streets, and medical helicopters roared overhead in the sky. The city of Jerusalem had suffered major damage which had altered many lives, and reconfigured the natural landmarks. Nothing would ever be the same again, of that Lily was certain.

She thought of Dan and Eli living in the Armenian Quarter of the Old City. She fervently hoped their neighborhood had not been leveled by the quake. She would find them. Perhaps they could explain the cryptic message about the scarlet thread.

Chapter 35

Lily found the brothers at home, unhurt but in a highly agitated state. Dan paced the floor, wringing his hands like an old woman while he listened to the latest report on the radio. He occasionally stopped and repeated what he was hearing. "Christ Church has been spared but the Scottish Hospice has been leveled." Then he did some more distracted pacing before exclaiming, "The YMCA buildings are demolished, but across the street, the King David is still standing."

Eli, more in control of his nerves but nevertheless looking pale and haggard, directed Lily to sit on the sofa. Too distraught to offer refreshments, he had the composure of mind to ask if Abigail and Ari were safe.

"Abigail is in Ain Karem. The quake did no damage there."

"Ari is there also?" Dan asked, still visibly agitated.

Lily, trying to keep a grip on her emotions but failing, blurted out, "He's underground somewhere, with Scott."

"You haven't heard from him? That's not like Ari. He would try to contact you if he could."

"Neither of us have mobile phones," Lily admitted.

Dan stopped long enough to give Lily a one-armed hug of consolation. She smiled ruefully in acknowledgment of his gesture. "I believe they're all right." She looked at her hands, suddenly feeling awkward about speaking of her fragile faith. "Sister Angelica seems convinced they've come to no harm."

"Well, there you have it," Eli interjected, "out of the mouth of two witnesses."

"Whatever," Lily mumbled, feeling her face flush with embarrassment. She pushed some loose curls off her forehead then delicately cleared her throat. "I've actually come here about something else."

Both the brothers paused with a look of puzzlement on their faces. "Go on," Eli responded.

Lily deliberately folded her hands in her lap to keep them from trembling. She spoke slowly, enunciating each word as if English was not her mother tongue. "I found myself praying to *Yeshua HaMashiach*. That's after getting no response from the angel Michael or, you know, *HaShem*." She looked up to see their reaction and continued when she saw no negative response in their demeanor. "So I asked *Yeshua* to help Ari and Scott, wherever they are."

"And?" The brothers said simultaneously, with the beginning of a smile on their lips.

"I got nothing, no response, although I felt strangely peaceful. Then I received the impression of something that sounded like *the scarlet thread*."

Dan and Eli hugged each other. Lily looked on in amazement, half expecting them to high-five each other in their enthusiasm. "What does it mean?"

Dan deferred to his brother, who now spoke in a controlled, steady voice. "Lily, I'm amazed and humbled by the goodness of the Lord in revealing this to you." He looked meaningfully at his brother before continuing, "Especially in these terrible circumstances. Jerusalem will never be the same after today. And neither will our lives. We talked to you recently about establishing a refuge in the Negev. The time has come."

Lily nodded her head impatiently. "I'm willing to join you, with Ari of course, but what about this red string thing?"

"I'm getting to that," Eli said, with less enthusiasm than Lily thought warranted. "First of all, it's not really a red string, such as movie stars wear on their wrists thinking they're following the Kabala."

"Like Madonna?" Lily wrinkled her nose in distaste.

Eli refused to even acknowledge the singer. "The scarlet thread is a theological term, if you like. We don't have time, under the circumstances, to give you a complete explanation, but it will suffice to say this particular scarlet thread is a symbol God has used from the time of Cain and Abel, down through the history of the Jews, culminating in the cross of Jesus Christ. It represents blood, more specifically a blood sacrifice."

Lily pursed her lips and remained silent, while Dan added to her puzzlement by adding, "Without blood, there is no sacrifice, and without the atonement, there is no salvation. It's that simple."

"I suppose I will understand in time, but right now it isn't making much sense to me."

"Don't worry, that's the word the Lord gave you, and he will make it perfectly clear, if not today, in the future. In the meantime, what can we do to find Ari?"

"I know he's somewhere underground in the City of David. Will you go with me now?" Lily looked expectantly from one to the other.

Without a moment's hesitation they agreed to the search. Eli, the practical one, suggested they take flashlights and a rope, and for good measure tucked bandages into his shirt pocket. Dan paused at the open door, looked up to heaven, and asked the Lord to give them grace to face whatever they found.

Lily harrumphed with mild annoyance. "I told you Ari and Scott have come to no harm."

Dan seemed to take no offense, and offered his arm to Lily in a gesture of friendship. "Never hurts to ask for grace."

They made their way down the narrow lane in the Armenian Quarter, marveling at the way the earthquake had snaked its way across the landscape, missing entire neighborhoods and leveling others. As they neared the Temple Mount, the number of police, soldiers, and first responders multiplied. The Western Wall was still standing, miraculously, as Dan pointed out, but many worshippers had been hurt by falling rocks and even boulders.

"God only knows how many are lying dead under the collapsed mosque," Lily murmured.

The plaza was blocked by the army, ambulances, and police jeeps which prevented them from getting to the Dung Gate. Eli took charge and led them back up the stairs to the Jewish Quarter. From there they made their way through the parking lot to the Valley of Hinnom.

"Okay, we're going to have to stay off the road and make our way down the slope of Mount Zion. There is an ancient stepped street here, very seldom used." Eli then warned them, "Watch out for open graves."

Lily stopped in her tracks. "What do you mean open graves?" She felt like screaming but managed to exercise self-control and shut her mouth again.

Dan took her elbow and urged her on. "It's biblical, Lily. The graves might have opened during the quake." His words did not reassure her, and now she remembered how much she hated this side of the Old City. She immediately became alert, hoping she would not see that image of a black, menacing shadow she identified as Lucifer. She even turned her head upwards and sniffed the air. Dan gave her a quizzical look, but Eli motioned them to hurry.

After slipping and sliding on the ancient stone steps, they made it to the bottom of the slope, and stopped to stare at what remained of the neighborhood of Silwan. Most of the houses were nothing more than flimsy shelters put up over the years by squatters and they now lay in ruins. Those residents who had escaped with their lives had instinctively run to the Greek owned garden where no building could fall on them. They stood, wailing, with vacant eyes, overwhelmed by the disaster. Lily put her hand to her mouth in commiseration. She turned to the brothers and whispered, "This is the very garden where Ari remained hidden for many months."

Just speaking his name put steel in her spine, and she pointed to the partially excavated pool of Siloam. "That's the lower entrance to the City of David. There's the gate house, still standing." She pointed with her arm in the direction of the little one-man shed. "I know how to get into the caverns from here. Follow me."

Eli appeared relieved to let Lily lead the way as they circumvented the crowded garden and made their way to the gatehouse. Quickly bypassing the shallow pool, which contained dark green stagnant water, they ran up the stone steps, still in place since the time of the Second Temple. They hadn't gone far before they reached a dead-end.

Eli stood and stared at the steel girders. "This is what kept this portion from caving in during the quake."

"Yeah," Lily responded, "Lots of those down here." She glanced over her shoulder. "The dry tunnel to the left leads deep underground and should come out just above a large cavern, which may have been a cistern. It's all a bit confusing, but I think Scott said he would core for pollen in one of these recently excavated cisterns."

Lily took off at a fast pace and only stopped to get her bearings and wait for Dan and Eli to catch up. She knew her long legs gave her an advantage, plus the fact that she was at least ten years younger.

Panting with the exertion, Eli stopped and bent over with his hands on his knees. "I hope you are not taking us through the Siloam tunnel. I can't bear dark, narrow passages, especially if they're full of water."

Lily acknowledged his phobia with a shake of her head. "Nope, this way is just a hundred meters and dry."

But when they reached the end of the tunnel they found the entrance to the cavern blocked by fallen boulders and loose rubble. They stood in the semi-darkness with only their flashlights for illumination. Time appeared to have stopped deep in the bowels of the earth. Except for their own raspy breathing, they heard nothing. This did not feel like the calm quiet of a clear summer day. This was the silence of the grave. The air smelled like the scent of decayed spices and damp earth in a sealed tomb.

Eli suggested they retrace their steps and go back. Dan and Lily reluctantly agreed they could go no farther. Lily was now in the rear. Disappointment made her wearily drag her feet. She let the brothers get far ahead of her in the dark tunnel. The glow from her flashlight cast weird shadows on the wall and low ceiling, and she let her mind wander. Cold and fatigue added to her state of mental stupor causing her to be caught off-guard by a sound like a woodpecker tapping on a pole. She tried to rationalize what she thought she heard. *There can't be any birds down here. I must be hallucinating.* But there it was again, tap, tap, and tap. In desperation and mild insanity she also tapped with her flashlight on the wall of the tunnel. To her surprise she heard a responding tap.

"Hey you guys, come back," she yelled to the brothers. "I've found them."

Chapter 36

The three rescuers quickly came to the conclusion they did not have the tools or the muscles to chisel through solid rock. Lily refused to leave the tunnel, stating she would keep tapping to reassure Ari and Scott they were not alone. Dan volunteered to stay with Lily. Eli left to run back for help. Lily insisted he try to reach Pincus by phone.

"Trust me. The Mossad has resources you can only imagine." She hastily recited a phone number and access code, and then made Eli repeat it until he had it memorized. "Tell Pincus where we are and to bring what we need to extricate Ari and Scott."

"What if someone else answers?" Eli asked, his forehead wrinkling with anxiety.

"Only Pincus answers this number. It's just for emergencies."

"Like now," Dan added, putting a reassuring hand on his brother's arm. "Go quickly, and the Lord help you."

* * * *

Eli retraced his steps through the tunnel, ran past the Siloam pool and out to the lane that continued down to Ein Rogel. He paused to catch his breath, and made the decision not to take the steep steps back up Mount Zion. He hoped the emergency personnel by the Western Wall would have mobile phones.

Sirens blasted his ears as he approached the Dung Gate. Traffic stood at a standstill, as a panicked population tried to get out of Jerusalem. Ambulances and police cars wrangled with private sedans. Irate drivers shouted at one another, and argued with Border Patrol officers. No one was moving in either direction.

Eli ran up to an ambulance driver who stood beside the open door of his vehicle, shaking his head, as he lit a cigarette. "Got a phone I can use?" Eli shouted. The man looked at him with a blank stare, tossed his half-smoked cigarette to the pavement before replying, "Won't help if I did. Phone service is down all over the city." He casually stepped on the still-burning butt. "What's your emergency?"

Eli licked his dry lips before responding. "My friends are trapped underground." He motioned with his head towards the City of David Excavation Park.

"Tourists?"

"No, Israeli archaeologists."

The man's eyes lit with interest. "How many?"

"Two men are barricaded under the debris, and my brother and another friend are standing watch until I return with help. I have a special number to call if only I can get to a phone." Eli's voice broke with a half sob.

"Well, I don't know what kind of special connection you think you have, but there are Shin Bet agents up there by the entrance to the Temple Mount. No telling what kind of protests the Arabs are going to pull at this stage." He smiled slyly, and added, "Their mosque is toast."

"Thanks," Eli replied, not knowing quite how to respond. He certainly did not wish the Palestinians more grief than they already were experiencing today. "It's worth a try." He turned and made his way through the crowd, weaving in and out with as much speed as he could manage. He found the way in more accessible than the way out, as people tried to leave the area.

Near the ramp which led up to the Temple Mount, Eli saw a small contingent of special agents, identifiable by the loose jackets concealing their handguns. He cautiously approached and made eye contact with the nearest one.

"Excuse me for bothering you, but I need to speak with someone at this number." He slowly recited the number Lily gave him, hoping she knew what she was doing.

Before he finished reciting the number, the agent's face changed from open and friendly to instantly on guard. "Who gave you that prefix?" he barked in anger.

"Well, my friend Lily did," Eli truthfully stammered, shaken by the hostility he heard in the man's voice.

"Who the hell is Lily?"

"It's her husband trapped underground."

"Why this number?"

"She said it was only to be used in emergencies. That's all I know." Eli stood his ground, acting braver than he felt.

"Wait here." The agent walked a few paces to another agent, spoke to him, nodded, and then returned.

"Give me the complete number again. I'll place the call on my mobile."

Eli recited the number again, and waited patiently while the man punched it in. He heard the agent identify himself as soon as someone on the other end picked up. He heard him say Lily's name.

"*Kakh*, here take it." The man handed him the mobile phone. Eli held it to his ear.

"Pincus, speaking, what can I do for you?"

Eli's mouth was now so dry he could hardly speak, but he managed to croak, "Ari and Scott are trapped underground."

"Precisely where?" Pincus asked.

"City of David excavations. Lily and my brother are standing by. They came in through the tunnel near the Siloam pool. You know where it is?"

"I can find it. Tell Lily to wait there. I'll send help."
The phone went dead, and Eli handed it back to the agent
who looked at him strangely.

"*Besedar,* is everything all right?"

"I don't know," Eli mumbled. "I have to go." Without
another word he ran back to the Siloam Pool and through
the dry tunnel once again. He found Lily and Dan where
he'd left them.

"Did you reach Pincus?" Lily's voice rose hysterically
high.

"He said he will send help, whatever that means." Eli
squatted on his heels to rest.

Dan patted his brother on the shoulder in affirmation of
a job well done. "Stay with Lily. I'll wait at the entrance to
guide them in."

* * * *

The time passed in slow increments, marked only by
the sound of tapping coming from the other side of the
tunnel wall. Lily muttered under her breath, "This is the
last time I ever want to be underground."

Eli mentioned Ari was probably vowing the same
thing. That comment made Lily laugh despite herself.
"Yeah, but I bet Scott will continue working here."

"Of course, this is his profession."

When Lily was about to lose heart and give up on help
arriving, she heard the sound of more than one person
approaching through the tunnel. "They're here," she said,
almost giddy with relief.

Motti Pincus appeared first, hunched over due to his
height and the low ceiling. Behind him followed two men,
one with a jack hammer, and the other with a pickaxe.
Without any unnecessary words or movements, he studied
the situation and commanded they break through the wall.

As he motioned to his team to get on with it, he turned to Lily, standing behind him in the narrow, dark tunnel.

"I tried to reach Ronnie Evron, the lead investigator of this site. He's apparently out of the country." Pincus coughed discreetly. "I take full responsibility for any damage we might do." Lily gave him a thankful nod.

Two hours later, they made an opening in the wall large enough for Ari and Scott to crawl through, tired, bruised, and dirty, but grateful to be alive. Later, as they sat recuperating under the leafy fig tree by the Siloam pool, details of what Scott and Ari had discovered started to come out.

Pincus pursed his lips and whistled softly when he heard mention of the cave containing the tomb of a king. "This information must remain secret. We anticipate a diplomatic and possibly a military attack at any time. Our Arab neighbors undoubtedly will blame us for the destruction of the mosque. Somehow, we control earthquake activity, you know."

Ari wiped the dirt off his face with a wet handkerchief, and looked at Scott with pity. "Now is the wrong time to announce you found King David's burial cave. It would appear to be further evidence of our right to Jerusalem as our capital."

Pincus stared hard at both Scott and Ari. "My team will seal off the tunnel with explosives, and blame it on the earthquake. I'll see to it that the Antiquities Department is informed."

Scott, who had said little up to this point, sat there with cuts and scratches on his face and hands, and mumbled something under his breath.

"What's that?" Pincus spoke more sharply than he intended.

"The sarcophagus will not walk away. It will still be there when the time is more appropriate." Scott smiled weakly. "Anyway, it will be a long time before work begins here again. I take it Jerusalem has been significantly damaged?"

"Catastrophic," Pincus answered tightlipped. "By the way, Ari, I was overseeing the damage to the American Colony Hotel when I got Lily's message." He peered directly into Ari's bruised face. "Your brother is among the dead."

Lily audibly gasped and turned to see Ari's reaction.

A look of relief gradually spread over her husband's features, beginning with his eyes and spreading to the down-turned corners of his lips. "I wanted to kill him."

Pincus's cheek muscle twitched involuntarily. "Well, his death now releases you from the hold he had on you, doesn't it?" Ari mutely nodded. Pincus then slowly rubbed his hands together before adding, "The earthquake wiped out Reza's entire network in one beautiful stroke of nature."

"All of them dead?" Ari asked, stunned.

Pincus nodded. "Looks like Reza convened a confab in his hotel room. We're still trying to identify names and nationalities."

Lily put her arms around Ari and held him tightly. The others looked away in embarrassment as the couple's tears of relief mingled freely. "It's finally over," Lily murmured.

Ari lifted his head and stared across the pool. "The Mahdi died in the earthquake," he said emphatically.

"Right," Pincus said, with a knowing nod. "A full report of the fatal injuries he sustained at the American Colony will be made known to all the relevant parties."

Epilogue

Six months later

The ancient walls of Jerusalem lie desolate, the building stones haphazardly tossed about by the force of the earthquake. It will take years to restore what was destroyed in just a few minutes. The Al Aqsa Mosque on the Temple Mount will never again be a house of worship. The faithful Muslims, fearing aftershocks, prefer to pray in the underground mosque beneath the sacred grounds. This subterranean man-made cave received no damage, and there they feel safe. The damage on the Mount of Olives is extensive, but the Intercontinental Hotel is already being rebuilt. In West Jerusalem, the YMCA complex did not fare so well, and there is no money readily available to rebuild. The Church of Scotland recently voted to sell their damaged property in Jerusalem, washing their hands of any involvement in the Zionist State.

Professor Scott continues his research in the City of David, but he carefully avoids excavating anywhere near the cave he and Ari found. He guards his field notebook with the carefully written description of what they discovered. He knows the time will come when he can return to the secret burial cave, and he anticipates it will be the climax of his career.

Ari and his family, living under assumed names provided by the Mossad, have joined Eli and Dan on their farm in the Negev. It is a stretch of the imagination to call it a farm, for little grows there in the searing heat. They do have a deep artesian well which supplies the small community with enough water for drinking and bathing.

Recycled water keeps a small vegetable garden alive, as well as a few fruit trees and the grape arbor in the courtyard.

Abigail is now walking, but mostly runs. She talks non-stop in both English and Hebrew. Her playmates, somewhat older, are the children of the fisherman, Shimon. He and his wife have come to dwell in the desert with their sons, Barak, Raam, and Lev, plus their six daughters. All the children, whose complexions are turning deep brown from the intense sun, are adapting to their new environment with abandon. Ari calls them his desert rats.

The members of the Mahdi Brotherhood, not killed in the earthquake, still gather in Damascus to determine what should be done about the Hidden Imam. Some think Ari is an imposter, but cannot prove their case. Others, including Abd Umar, maintain the Mahdi has done what he historically has always done. After disappearing into thin air, the Holy One will appear again at the set time.

Ari has determined to put the past behind him and diligently helps with the food supply for the little community. In addition to keeping a mother goat with two kids, he tends sixteen red hens, and one rooster. Ari has purchased an Arabian mare, which he rides into the desert in the early hours of the morning. On his solitary sojourns through the rocky sage, he ponders the strange path his life has taken. He does not know what the future will bring, but he is content with the present.

* * * *

Daniel and Eliahu continue to spend their mornings in prayer or meditation. In the evenings, after the supper dishes are washed, dried and put away, they hold a Bible study in the sitting room. Attendance is always optional. Their community has few rules. The one constant in their ordinary routine of daily life is the unmistakable current of expectation.

Every morning Lily watches her husband ride off before dawn. She intuitively knows he needs this time to heal, as well as to grow spiritually. Lily has no further encounters with the archangel Michael. Like Ari's Mahdi role, her calling to speak with angels is on hold. She marvels at Abigail's ability to speak a mile a minute in two languages. She wonders what gifts her daughter will inherit.